WITHDRAWN

Go, Team, Go!

JOHN R. TUNIS

Go, Team, Go!

William Morrow & Company, Inc.
New York   *1954*

192249

Ninth Printing, August, 1966

Copyright, 1954, by Lucy R. Tunis
Printed in the United States of America
All rights reserved. Published simultaneously in the
Dominion of Canada
by George J. McLeod Limited, Toronto.
Library of Congress Catalog Card No. 54-5520

"The development of people is the first concern of a democracy."

David E. Lilienthal

Go, Team, Go!

Chapter 1

The huge bus rocked through the misty March night. Some of that first high elation had worn off, some of the delirious joy had gone now, for the gang was sleepy with dinner and exhausted emotionally and physically from the long, wearying day. So the noise and shouting were dying away. Suddenly there was a bang, a kind of explosion, from the front of the bus. The Davis twins on the B team had passed a trick cigar to the driver and even helped him light it, too.

Again shouts and laughter echoed up and down the car. "Them kids! They're something," remarked Red, yanked from a drowse.

"Yeah," said Little Tom, in the seat beside him, peering up the aisle. "Yeah, they're really something, aren't they? They'd be just the same if we lost, too."

"Sure would," agreed his teammate promptly.

As they settled back in their seats a piercing

9

scream came from far ahead up the road. It pene-
trated the interior of the bus, growing louder and
louder.

"Police escort! That must be the squad car,"
everyone said.

"Uh-huh, that's the police escort."

Nobody was much surprised. Everyone expected
it. Everyone knew the town would greet its winning team that way. Naturally, they thought. Of
course they'd send out a police escort now we've
won the State.

The pneumatic brakes caught hold, the red and
white streamers attached to the outside of the bus
fluttered down, and with a hiss and another hiss
the big vehicle slurred to a stop. Behind, the three
buses with the girls of Block R, the Ridgewood
cheering section, also came to a halt. The long
procession stood waiting for the approaching siren,
moving toward them through the fog. Soon it was
near, it was alongside. They yelled and shouted as
Jack Curtis, the police chief, turned, backed his gray
sedan, and with the siren all out moved to the head
of the procession.

The noise increased as they reached the outskirts
of town, and the final mile was through a long line
of horn-sounding cars parked on both sides of the
road. At Courthouse Square the team disembarked,
put on firemen's hats and slickers, and climbed up

on the big hook and ladder for the traditional ride through the city.

The community was welcoming back its conquering heroes, victors for the first time in the State Basketball Tournament at Indianapolis. This would be a reception nobody would ever forget. No one, least of all the team, ever did forget it, either. Because its effect on the lives of those boys and, in fact, on the lives of every citizen from the mayor down, brought consequences the town of Ridgewood, Indiana, would always remember.

Chapter 2

Although it was nearly two o'clock, and usually in Ridgewood folks went to bed and dragged the sidewalks in at nine, the high-school gymnasium was as packed that morning as if Ridgewood had been playing Marbletown, its greatest and most hated rival. Round the balcony folks were standing six deep, the floor was filled with standees, and the only empty spot in the bleachers was the section in the middle reserved for the girls of Block R.

While the team had been taken round to the raging bonfire in the park, Block R came directly to the gym. There they were, coming in now, scrambling and shoving and pushing down to their seats, a colorful sight in their red skirts and white sweaters. They had been going for over fourteen hours, ever since they piled into the buses shortly before ten that morning in front of the high school. They had yelled and shouted and cheered all afternoon and evening, yet they were still a vibrant, lively group—even, without leaders or direction, breaking spontaneously into a yell, one row swinging to the left, the other to the right as they shouted.

"Let's go . . . big team . . . let's go. . . ."

Two hundred and fifty pairs of hands smacked together, two hundred and fifty voices screamed. "Let's go . . . big team . . . let's go!"

"Indianapolis, here we are . . . with the greatest team by far!"

Then with a sudden cry they rose to their feet. The noise deafened everyone in the big gymnasium, defied all sense, swept up all those thousands into one great roar of sound. For the team was coming up on the platform.

Hysterically the crowd rose too, waving toward them. They shambled to the front row of seats, no longer bare-legged giants in red shirts and white shorts but tall, awkward boys in windbreakers and slacks, shirts open at the neck, chiefly composed of arms and feet which they didn't know what to do with. They stood, hands in their pockets, then behind their backs, embarrassed by the reception, yet radiant, too, as they looked down at the adulating crowd. They were a typical bunch of Hoosiers, the team: the son of the mayor, the son of the most notorious bookmaker in the county, the son of the town's leading manufacturer, the son of the night watchman in the Chrysler plant, the

son of the Methodist minister—each on that platform
for a single reason, because he had earned his spot
on the basketball team that had won the State.

Little Tom McWilliams, six feet four and a
bad man under that basket, stood happily yet
somewhat uncomfortably in the front row. He
watched the yell leaders rush out: two boys in white
sweaters with big red *R's* on them and white pants,
two girls in white sweaters and white skirts. The
good-looking one was Mary Jo Berry, his own, his
girl. He tried hard not to watch her, as he had tried
hard all afternoon and evening to concentrate on
the man he was guarding; he tried to look out at
the crowd, at the sea of faces, many of which were
familiar. But it was minutes before they quieted
down, and Little Tom, like the others, had to stand
there looking foolish, now on one foot, now on the
other. But when a town wins its first State, somehow
it tastes extra good because of the years of waiting,
and folks, he knew, wanted to show their pleasure.

At last, to their relief, the boys were permitted
to subside into the long row of chairs. Just behind
them was another row and somewhere back there,
Tom knew, was his father, probably as proud and
happy as anyone in the gym. Finally the principal
came forward, said a few words into the mike which
in the general confusion were hard to hear, turned,

and held out his hand to a figure working his way through the rows of chairs.

The mayor came up front, a big man, a bear of a figure. He was called Big Tom to distinguish him from his son, who was now as famous as his father. Or more so. Because anyone can be mayor of an Indiana town, but only five boys in the whole state can be members of the championship basketball team.

The crowd greeted the mayor warmly, almost affectionately, as he stood handling the mike, running one hand through his mane of black hair, beaming on them. And when he raised his arm, silence fell immediately. They listened.

"Friends . . . I'm mighty proud, as you can imagine . . . I'm mighty proud tonight . . . I figgered when the Citizen's Committee nominated me . . . when I was elected mayor . . . it was the happiest day of my life . . . I was wrong. This is."

He was interrupted by a burst of noise, cheers, hand clapping; but again he raised his hand, again silence immediately descended.

"I'd like to explain just why I'm so proud. Maybe you wouldn't guess the real reason. Sure I'm proud we won the State for the first time. Naturally I'm proud because my boy is on the team. But what makes me proudest is because I *know* . . . if Hooks Barnum picked Tom to play forward on the Ridgewood Redskins, he won his place strictly on his own."

Again the cheers broke out, spontaneous, drowning the words of the speaker. You could see that everyone in town liked and respected the mayor.

"Folks . . . tonight it's an honor and a pleasure for me to introduce to you the greatest coach in the state of Indiana . . . and, of course, that means in the whole United States . . . Hooks . . ."

The crowd went wild. The varsity, the B team, and the substitutes rose yelling as the short, sturdy man worked his way up front. He was thick through the shoulders, with the thin waist of the former athlete; there was gray in the hair around his ears, and his face was gray and drained. Everyone could see plainly what this man had suffered and endured in the hours of this long day. He came toward the mike, took it, looked out at the raging crowd, started to speak, said something unheard in the noise, and was suddenly surrounded.

The boys, unable to restrain themselves, forgot they were on the platform before six thousand celebrating townspeople. Breaking ranks, pushing back their chairs, they all made for the man beside the mike, surrounding him, hugging him, slapping his back, his arms, showing their affection for the one person who from the start had believed in them, who even in early November had told them they could win the State.

It was three in the morning before the principal

started to close the meeting with an announcement about the P-rade to be held downtown on Monday afternoon and the dinner at the Quarterbacks Club in the evening, at which gold wrist watches with the score of the finals and their names engraved on the back would be presented to every member of the team. Then he mentioned the rally in the school auditorium on Tuesday morning and finally got round to the statement they all wanted to hear. Yes, school would be closed on Monday.

With a long, last, mighty roar, the crowd broke up. Block R dissolved toward the exits in the stands while the team, coming down from the platform, had to fight their way across the floor through a sea of congratulating parents, schoolmates, businessmen, friends, and folks they didn't know. Little Tom, after considerable effort, reached the main door, worked through to the steps outside and, not seeing the person he was looking for, stood waiting, shaking hands with everyone who could push up to him.

"Thanks . . . thanks lots . . . Jimmie . . . yeah, thanks, Mis' Reynolds . . . yeah, we'll all be back next year . . . thanks . . . gee, thanks, Sally . . . thanks, Jack . . . thanks, kid . . . thanks, Mr. Freeman . . . well, you never know about next year, but the whole team will be back . . . thanks, Mac . . . thanks . . . yep, we sure were lucky that last

quarter . . . yeah, I felt we'd win all along, Harry
. . . thanks, Fred boy, thanks lots."

He towered over the crowd and from his great
height searched the people still streaming through
the open doors. Surely she would come. Surely she
would want to get to him at once; surely she
wouldn't have left yet. She must be coming out
soon. For it was not his family he was looking for
at that moment but someone he had hardly seen
during the last, feverish week of practice for the
finals.

Hours seemed to pass, the crowd poured endlessly
by, until finally he caught sight of her in the door,
tossing her blond hair, her big eyes searching for
him, the white sweater with the red *R* plainly visible. Then she saw him, waved one hand, and started
to shove through the crowd to his side. He pushed
aside the circle of kids who were replaying the last
minutes of the game. As she came near, she jumped
toward him. He grasped her under the shoulders,
yanked her off her feet, and into his arms.

For a long while she hung there, kissing him
furiously, while the crowd passing by turned and
stared. One small youngster gave a wolf whistle,
but several others turned on him.

"You creep! You sap! That's Mary Jo Berry, that
is. That's Little Tom's girl!"

Chapter 3

Ridgewood felt good that next fall. Why not? With the whole varsity back and the taste of victory in everyone's mouth, folks were sure the team would win the State again the following March. But to understand the situation, you must realize how the town felt toward Marbletown.

Ridgewood and Marbletown, forty miles apart, had always been great rivals and tough opponents in every sport. Whenever Ridgewood won a victory over Marbletown, it gave the town a little extra pleasure; if, on the other hand, the Ridgewood football or basketball team dropped a game to the Bearcats, it hurt. Actually, Ridgewood never had managed to beat them often in basketball until Hooks Barnum came to coach the high-school team.

Hooks Barnum was originally from Marbletown. Not only did he grow up and go to high school there, he played in the very first Bearcat basketball team to win the State. Then, returning eighteen years later as coach, he brought them another title, their first since he had been on the team himself. Naturally he was the town hero—to everyone save the superintendent of schools, who was jealous of him and refused Hooks the raise he asked for after winning the State for Marbletown. This cut him badly. Six months later he resigned and within twenty-four hours was hired by Ridgewood, whose team hadn't even won the sectionals for more years than anyone could remember.

Hooks Barnum was a strange, strong, independent character. Either people liked him or they didn't. He made no concessions to be popular—never went out of his way to handshake the important folks in town. He played no favorites, even when he put the mayor's son in at forward on his varsity team. He was always courteous and long-suffering with the imbeciles who asked the impossible (that is, tickets for the State), but he never played up to anyone or made a fuss over the members of the school board, as some coaches did.

In other words, Hooks treated everybody alike, young and old, in school and in town. The boys on his teams, however, all loved him. They appreciated, as no one else could, what he had accomplished in three years—how he worked with them and helped them whether they were on the B team or the varsity, not only as basketball players but as individuals with problems of their own.

Naturally it didn't take long for the entire school to discover this fact. After a while it got so that boys or girls went immediately to Hooks when they were in trouble and seldom to the dean.

Within three seasons his coaching and his character began to have an effect, as the character of a good man always does in sport. Then the Redskins finally won the State, and for the first time Ridgewood had a championship basketball team. That next fall, with his varsity and most of the B team back, everyone in town was sure they would have another winner. In fact, they counted on it so much that already, it was said, bets were being made downtown that Ridgewood would take the State again. The town had drunk the heady wine of victory and unanimously decided that it tasted mighty good.

But Hooks knew he had a problem on his hands. From the start of practice he realized he faced almost as much of a task as he had in building up a winner in a school that had become accustomed to defeat and had even begun to accept it.

"This won't be easy," he told the squad. "This is tough; this is going to be grim for us. There's a long, rocky road ahead, and every single team on the schedule from the start will be gunning for us. It won't be enough to be as good as last year. We've got to be better. If anyone gets complacent," he warned them again and again, "if anyone thinks we can coast in, he's wrong, dead wrong."

There were others in town who saw the problem too, and one of them was the mayor. Little Tom McWilliams pounded down the stairs one night in November to find his father in his chair, reading the *Evening Sentinel* as usual.

He glanced up and observed that his son had on a necktie and a clean suit. "Dressed up tonight, aren't you, Tom? What is it, another dance?"

The tall boy with the crew haircut frowned. "Gee, Dad, I haven't time for women nowadays. I'm too busy. This is the night of the Service Club's dinner for the team."

"Oh, I see. You've got a necktie on, so I figgered . . . Say, wasn't the Service Club dinner last week?"

"Nope, that was the Chamber of Commerce dinner at the Mansion House."

"I see. What's cooking next week?"

Little Tom missed the slightly ironical flavor of his father's tone. "Next week? The Kiwanis. They're going to present gold medals to us guys on the team."

"Huh! You chaps better watch out. You'll get so fat attending banquets you won't be able to play basketball. Or do any work in school, either."

"Aw, that's the last one. Don't worry. Hooks Barnum knows what he's doing all the time."

"Yes, but do you boys—"

"Sure we do. Dad, know what?"

The mayor picked up the *Sentinel*, quite evidently listening with only half an ear to his tall son standing there before him. "Say on," he replied casually.

"There's a pool on us to hit the finals again, a big pool. Seven thousand six hundred bucks, and growing fast."

The *Sentinel* fell to the floor. Big Tom yanked off his glasses and looked up. "No! You mean that? Seven thousand you'll win the State? They're crazy!"

"Dad! I knew you weren't listening to what I said. You never pay attention. It isn't seven thousand, it's seven thousand six hundred right now. And it isn't to *win;* it's that the team will reach the finals. And the pool is growing fast; they expect it will be fifteen thousand, end of this month."

"*They* do? Who does? How d'you know?"

Little Tom hesitated, not liking to give away a friend. Besides, he realized that his father knew just exactly where he got his information. So he said nothing.

Big Tom went on, with some annoyance in his voice. "Why, they're crazy, those men! That's why we have trouble—installment sales hard to collect, credit getting tight. Most of those fellows can't afford to lose money. It's wrong. I'd just like to clean out that joint—lock, stock, and barrel."

Little Tom understood his father meant Mac and Joe's Bar and Grill on Indiana Avenue, where a lot of the betting in town took place. It was here that old Sam Blake, father of Red, Tom's teammate, and the town's leading bookie, was usually to be found any afternoon about two.

Tom couldn't resist suggesting to his father, "Why don't you then? You're the mayor. It it's all wrong, why don't you have Jack Curtis raid the place and lock him up?"

"Because it wouldn't accomplish anything, that's why. We'd have to get the goods on him, see the money pass, and even if we did he'd be out on bail in ten minutes. Then six weeks later his case would come up and he'd be fined twenty-five bucks. What's that? An hour later he'd be back taking bets in Mac's Grill again. That's exactly why we don't do anything." He shoved the paper away, rose and lighted a cigarette, and walked across the room nervously. "Seven thousand . . . I know some of the men in that pool . . . half of them have no business betting. They can't afford to lose. They live on a margin. They're crazy!"

"They might win, Dad," Little Tom remarked complacently. It was evident that Hook's warning had not shaken his confidence in the team to any extent.

"Sure. Granted. Might lose, too. Then what? Son, you boys are a long ways from hitting the finals. You have a job ahead of you, a big job."

"Aw, Dad, we have the whole varsity back again, haven't we? We played together all last year."

"Sure you did. But you beat Fort Wayne by only two points and most of their varsity is back again too."

"We'll trim those guys the best day they ever had."

"Mebbe so. What about the Wildcats? You had a real battle with them. You were seven points down at the half."

"We won, didn't we?" His complete assurance was irritating to his father.

"You won, you won, sure you won. That isn't saying you will this year, though."

"Aw, Dad, you were a gloom all last winter. We came through all right then. We will again."

His father shook his paper, seeing he had made no dent in his son's complacence. Then his mother spoke. "Tom, please come home and get some sleep after the dinner. You were out last night and the night before. Please don't go round to Mary Jo's; she needs her sleep too, you know."

"Aw, gee, Mother," he said.

They treated him like a ten-year-old. After all, what's the most important thing in Ridgewood? Why, the basketball team. Right—the basketball team. And he was one of the two most vital members, the stopper, the set-shot expert, who pulled them together when they hit a losing streak. Anyhow, that's what Slim Harris, the sports editor of the *Sentinel*, called him. And he was the one who had chucked in the winning bucket that night before 16,000 maniacs in the field house at Indianapolis. Couldn't take that away from him.

Yet there they were, his family, treating him like a kid, telling him to come home early and all that stuff.

He grabbed his jacket and cap indignantly from the hall closet and went out the door and down the porch steps. Of course he was going over to Mary Jo's after the dinner; naturally he would want to tell her about it. Gosh, when the season starts and the games begin, a fellow can't go running round town at night. Not with Hooks Barnum as coach, he can't.

Chapter 4

Tom looked at him quickly. Somehow this was a new Hooks Barnum, a different person from the friend they had all known and loved the previous year. That afternoon in the gym he seemed almost more like a teacher than a friend. In fact, he sounded like Mr. Hitchcock, the principal, warning them in assembly that he would not tolerate roughhousing in the corridors after school.

They stood in a circle in the center of the floor as they had so many, many times before—Hooks and the varsity. Two or three were chewing gum nonchalantly, and Red Blake was bouncing a ball gently against the floor with one hand.

"Quit that, Red. I want your attention, all of you. Let's have quiet in here."

The tall boy, a basketball in his hands, looked at the coach with a slight frown on his forehead.

Hooks paid no attention and turned to Little Tom. "Tom, what's on tonight?"

He was surprised by the question. "Why, you mean . . . the Kiwanis deal, Hooks? They're giving gold medals to us guys on the varsity."

"When is the next banquet?" His query was crisp and brief.

"This is the last one, Hooks."

"Good. Now maybe we can get down to basketball. Maybe you guys will stop reading your clippings and tend to business. Oh, I know, I know. This is the start of the season, you haven't really got going yet; Harry Greathouse and Joe Boyd were playing football. I realize all that; but I'm telling you frankly, unless you fellows shake into it . . . Red!" He turned sharply toward the lanky center, who was tapping the ball gently on the floor again. The big boy straightened up, annoyed. His annoyance was less than the coach's. "Red, by this time you should know when I say quiet . . . I mean *quiet*."

The circle stood hushed, motionless. They had often seen him upset in games but never before in a practice session. Something was going wrong. At each end of the floor the boys on the B team were chucking in free throws and, as usual, above the stomp-stomp of feet and the slapping of the ball on the wooden floor, you could hear the shrill cries of the Davis twins. "Hey! Hey! Here, here, Randy!"

But the varsity, mouths open, eyes fixed on their coach, were uncomfortably silent.

"Tom!" Little Tom moved uneasily, feeling guilty for some reason, for no reason he could remember. "Tom, you were my playmaker last season; you set things up for us. This fall you've been slow and careless. You've all been careless—you especially, Red. Must be something on your mind; it sure isn't basketball. And you, Ned, you're shooting from way out. You know better'n that, all of you. You're making mistakes, that's why this B team is taking you. They will every time, too, unless you fellas snap out of it."

Wonder what's biting him, thought Little Tom. He talks like Dad. After all, we haven't been licked yet; we won sixteen straight and the State last year. What's he kicking about?

"You were the best-conditioned team in the tournament at Indianapolis; you had the legs, you could outrun anyone. That's why you took South Bend and Bosse in the finals. You went in to win and you did. I want you to get that attitude back, because this will be a tough year for us. After this Kiwanis deal tonight, I'm going to insist on strict training rules, same as we had in February and March—no late nights, no parties except on Saturdays."

A kind of sullen murmur ran round the circle. One boy's lips moved inaudibly in protest.

"How's that, Joe?"

"Oh, nothing, Hooks, nothing."

"Fine! Now you know. I'm not saying these things twice. I want you to make this practice good today. Some figure eights first off, a little shooting; then we'll scrimmage with the B team. Everyone on his toes, and see that every shot counts."

They turned, relieved, glad to be in action, to be moving, to be freed from his words.

"Let's go, let's go, gang . . . Yea, gang, let's go!"

Much later that afternoon, in the mellow dusk of late November, Tom and Red sat in Red's car at the curb outside Tom's home. The car was an ancient Chevvie which ran occasionally and, better still, was souped up so that when it did run it sounded like a jet plane. Folks two blocks away could tell Red's car.

At the moment, his feet on the dashboard, Red was studying the racing form sheet in that afternoon's Indianapolis *News*.

"Were you smart, fella, were you smart to get into this line! I wish I could think up something," said Tom, admiration in his voice. For you had to admit, even if you didn't exactly care for Red Blake, as some folks in town did not, that he was a businessman like his father. Red was the kind who would get ahead in life; he would succeed. He knew what he wanted and how to get it, too.

"Yeah, this guy Barnum. I hadda do something. Ya know, he treats us like kids this fall!"

"That's right," agreed Tom. "He's getting to sound like my old man telling me I shouldn't stay out late nights."

"Ain't it a fact!" said Red. "He's tough all of a sudden. When he tightened up, I hadda quit my job at the A. and P. That cost me eighteen bucks a week. Think he'll make it up? He will not!"

Indignation surged over Little Tom. "No! Hooks has no right to do that."

"Of course not. My old man says he's interfering with the free-enterprise system, that's what he's doing. Hooks just said the job was too much and to stop it. What's a guy to do? I need that dough; you can't make time with a girl nowadays unless you've got some cash."

"But how'd you learn, Red? How did you know what to do—where did you get wise to making a book?"

"My old man, he showed me. Besides, I been watching him make a book on the ball clubs and the races at Indianapolis for years. It's easy enough if you know how, if you play the percentages."

This wasn't quite clear, so Tom asked cautiously,

"You doing all right . . . you doing any good, are ya?"

Red turned scornfully. "Of course. Whatcha think I'm in it for—fun?"

"But the kids—if they keep on losing they won't bet, will they?"

"Some win; some lose," announced Red sagely. "Only I always win, see? I got the percentage in my favor; that's the whole secret of making a book. Last week I cleaned up . . . let me see." He fished a grimy notebook from the pocket of his wind-breaker, pulled off an elastic band, and opened it. The pages were barely visible in the dusk, filled as they were with figures. He went to work, adding up a column. "Let's see now . . . let's see . . . that's twenty . . . twenty-one . . . twenty-two sixty-five week before last . . . no, last week. This week . . . so far . . . I'm eighteen forty."

Naturally Tom was impressed. Who wouldn't be? There were the figures in black and white. You didn't have to break your back cutting lawns or raking leaves with somebody bossing you all day. You merely had to take bets from the kids and then add up your winnings at the end of the week.

"But aren't you afraid . . . if Barnum or old Hitchcock found out . . ."

"Nuts to them! I don't take bets or pay off on school property. I'm careful, I watch my step, see?

Believe me, I know my way round town. How can them guys get me?"

"Gee, if you ever lost that notebook . . ."

"Naw . . . I have another at home. I keep a copy of everything." More and more you had to admire him. He was a real businessman; he thought of everything. "And next week," he continued, "I'm set for a killing on the fight."

"The fight? What fight?"

"Yeah, dopey, the fight. Don'tcha ever read the papers? The lightweight championship, in Chicago —Kid Grindelwald against young Jeff Jones, the colored scrapper, on the twenty-fourth. You want in?" He opened his notebook to a page with half a dozen names and figures opposite them, his pencil ready. Little Tom could see why, as a businessman, he was so successful.

Tom thought hard. Baseball, yes, baseball he understood; but boxing and horse racing were unknown quantities. He needed money badly, because his time for outside work and his earning capacity had also been cut down by basketball practice every weekday.

However, he decided regretfully not to risk any cash. "Naw, I guess not. I don't know boxing."

"You don't need to; I do. C'mon, boy, I'll slap you into the pool. What say? This German can't lose. My old man knows; he saw the right people

in Chicago last week. The whole school is betting
on the colored boy; they'll lose their shirt. We'll
clean up and go down to a show at Indianapolis.
Nuts to Old Lady Barnum!"

Well, of course, if there was no risk at all, if
there was no danger of losing, why not?

"Can I come in for a buck, Red?" This was
really more than Tom cared to risk, yet anything
less might have sounded cheap.

"Sure, sure, whatever you say. Put you down for
a quarter if you say the word, only the more you
bet, the more you win." Red scribbled in the notebook, snapped back the elastic, and stuffed it in his
pocket.

"Tell ya what, Red. I'll give you the buck day
after tomorrow when my allowance is due. That
O.K.?"

Red turned on him. "Forget it, kid. You don't
need money with me, pal; your credit is good. Get
it? Besides, I tell ya, this thing is in the bag."

Chapter 5

The gang met Red Blake well down the street before school that morning. The gang consisted of the boys who had won on the fight and many of their interested and envious friends. They all knew Red never handed out cash on the school property, so they had gone down almost a block to greet him and get their winnings.

Little Tom was one of the group, although he had lost. He saw Red coming at last and knew at once from the expression on his face that he was in trouble. The crowd rushed toward him and surrounded him, and then moved slowly toward the school in a circle, all talking at once. From mouth to mouth, from the inside of the ring out, from the boys close to Red to those on the edge, who were less interested, the word passed in disgusted tones. "He hasn't got any dough."

"No money? How come he's got no money? Sure he has, he's got mine."

"Nope, he's busted."

"Hey, Jack, hey, Stinky, hey there, Harry! Red's got no money to pay off."

"Watcha mean he has no money? I paid him three bucks. I'll take it outa his hide."

But the fact was that no cash passed hands that morning after the Kid Grindelwald-Jeff Jones fight. Red Blake had learned the unpleasant lesson every bookmaker knows—that once in a while the public is right about something. Instead of betting evenly on the two contestants, the boys had mostly taken the long odds on Jones. Unfortunately Grindelwald, the favorite, had lost and Red was broke.

Now they had reached the stone walk leading to the school, and the gathering grew larger as the news spread and boy after boy came down from the steps to join the group. Inside, the warning bell sounded and then the first bell; but although they could be heard distinctly by the gang outside, no one paid any attention. They still stood there gesticulating and talking—all but Red Blake. Except for stating that he would return all the cash put up but could do nothing more, he remained silent and sullen. Unlike his experienced father, he had neglected to cover himself in case of an upset and was unable to meet his commitments.

It was nine o'clock now and the bell sounded sharply again, calling them to classes. They were in plain view from the dean's office on the second floor. Faces could be seen up there at the windows, watching them. Finally the dean came down the steps toward them. With reluctance the circle broke up, and the crowd slowly entered the building.

News spreads quickly in a school. Word got round fast in Ridgewood High during the morning that Red Blake wasn't going to be able to pay off on his book for the Grindelwald fight. Those who had lost were not at all disappointed by Red's promise to return their money, but they were in the minority. Those who had won, of course, were furious, and took no pains to conceal their anger.

By noon the principal discovered what had happened. After a long consultation with the dean, he summoned Red to his office. At one o'clock, the star center of the basketball team had been permanently dismissed from school for gambling.

Little Tom heard it soon afterward when he found Red cleaning out his locker, stunned and dismayed. A group of serious-faced boys were at his side.

When Tom learned the news he was as amazed as any of them. "But look, Red. . . . He can't fire you for that. You didn't bet on school property . . . you were careful. Why everyone in town bets . . . a little."

"He can't—only he has," replied Red grimly. "The little so-and-so!"

"Shoot, I'm gonna see him myself. I'll explain it, I'll set him right, I'll getcha back, Red. You wait and see." Tom knew these things happened sometimes and if they could be stopped before word got around the whole school, something might be done. So he went straight upstairs to the office of the principal. Mr. Hitchcock was still with the dean but received him immediately.

Tom explained the thing carefully. "See, Mr. Hitchcock, Red didn't cheat or anything. He's returning the kids' dough, every cent."

"I realize that, Tom. He explained that to me. But you must appreciate we can't have gambling going on here in school."

"Oh, he didn't gamble in school. He never passed money on the school property; he was careful about that."

"That's not the point. He took the boys' money for a book. He promoted gambling here in school. We don't allow that. Would your father approve of it, do you think?"

"Oh . . . he doesn't approve of lots of things . . . like the city council . . . and Democrats—"

Mr. Hitchcock interrupted hastily. "You think he approves of gamblers and gambling?"

Tom reflected, remembering his father's remarks

about Old Man Blake. "Well . . . he may not exactly approve, but he can't stop it. Why, everyone in town bets a little now and then, on a race or something. You know that, Mr. Hitchcock. All kinds of folks in town bet."

"What happens downtown is no concern of ours. This is a school. We're trying to make citizens, good citizens. We can't tolerate this sort of thing. This happened once before, when you were in junior high, I think, and we had to fire three boys for it. Red's no exception even if he is on the team."

Instantly Tom realized he had made a bad mistake, that he should have gone first to Hooks Barnum, who understood these things. Then Hooks could have taken on Mr. Hitchcock and straightened the whole thing out. For Hooks knew how disastrous it would be to lose his star center at the start of the season.

The coach was in his office in the gymnasium talking with Mr. Foster, the athletic director, and from the look on their faces Tom knew they had heard the bad news. This was a blow to the team and the team's chances of repeating last year's victory. If you lose one man you can usually find someone to take his place, but when your veteran center and best free-throw man is gone, your team is disrupted.

"You want me, Tom boy?"

"Yeah, Hooks. I guess you heard . . ."

"Yes, we were just talking about it."

Tom felt more hopeful. "What you gonna do, Hooks?" he asked eagerly.

The coach shook his head. "Not much we can do, Tom."

Tom was rocked now. That Mr. Hitchcock would be preachy, he expected. But that Hooks, who always saw things straight and clearly, would not put up a fight for Red at this moment, he couldn't understand. "Gee, Hooks, he hasn't really done anything wrong; he hasn't snitched any money or anything. He didn't do what that Rodenbaugh kid did last year and they let *him* off with a month's suspension. This isn't that bad. You know everyone in town bets; you know that, sure you do. Don't you, Mr. Foster?" He turned to the athletic director appealingly.

His mind went back to the World Series in October, when he had stood early one hot afternoon before a television set in Mac and Joe's Bar and Grill with Red Blake and Red's old man. In came Mr. Kennedy, a friend of his father's, the president of the Ridgewood Bank and Trust Company, to put a few dollars on the Yankees. Tom recalled his greeting to Old Man Blake.

"Hiya, Sam. How's it look?"

"Hiya, Glen. Four to three if you want the Yanks

right now." Sam Blake knew just about everyone in town and called them by their first names, too.

But now Hooks was firm, as firm as the principal. "No, Tom, there's nothing to do. Here in school we don't care what happens downtown; we have our standards and we have to live up to them. He was betting, Tom, keeping a book here in school, teaching the kids to gamble. We can't tolerate it."

"Aw, Hooks!" Here it was, more of the same, more of the bunk older folks handed out to young people. "Aw, Hooks, you don't need to be the mayor's son to know folks get away with anything they can. Red just got found out, that's all. It's not fair, it's not right, it's—"

"They get found out sooner or later, Tom. Things catch up with 'em like they did with Red. I know this is tough, it's hard for us all."

"But see here...." He could hardly believe Hooks would talk this way. He never had before. Always when a kid got into trouble—and plenty did in the course of a school year—Hooks saw the boy's angle and helped straighten things out. Yet on this important point, which meant the success of the whole season, he was siding with the old fossils who felt a guy was wrong to risk a quarter on a fight. And everybody knew there wasn't a businessman in town who wasn't aboard the pool for the team to hit the finals. Did they say that was wrong? Of course not!

No doubt about it, Tom felt—victory in the State had gone to the coach's head. Hooks Barnum was not the same. The year before he would have seen Red's angle and talked the principal into suspending him for a month, or a few weeks. While now he handed out the same line, the same old guff. . . .

"Look, Hooks," he pleaded, "this is Red's last year, his last chance; he's a senior."

"I know that. But by betting . . ."

"Betting! Why, the whole darn town bets. There's a room back of the Indiana Lunch with a board running across the entire wall that lists every track in America. I know. I've been in there; I've seen it. And there's punchboards in all the drugstores, and women and kids putting in their dimes and quarters. Isn't that betting, isn't it? Sure it is. We haven't anybody to replace him, Hooks. You know that."

"Son, I know it better than you do. We've been all over this before. Four years ago we threw a couple of kids out of school for the same thing; Red will have to take the consequences. What happens downtown has nothing to do with the school. You ought to know that; lots of things happen in town we don't allow here. We'll just have to get along with Strings Johnson from the B team."

"That clumsy ox!" Tom had a vivid picture of the six-foot-six colored boy stumbling over his own feet as he came down the floor. To be sure, he hadn't been so awkward lately in practice; but in a game he was useless.

Despair came over Tom at his inability to get these older people to quit preaching. After all, what did Red do? Only what his father did every day, only what everyone in town was doing.

When he returned to the crowd around the locker, Red looked at him anxiously over the circle of faces. "Whad' he say?"

"Aw, the same bunk they all hand out."

"You shoulda went to Barnum. He'll fix it."

"I did. Hooks is getting to be like the rest. Tell ya what, Red, I'll get my old man on the job. I'll get him working on it this afternoon. Believe me, one phone call to the school board and you'll see Hitchcock snap into it."

But the mayor was out of town that day. When the varsity took the floor against Central City before a full house in the evening, they had to play without their star center and pivot man, the boy who had scored eighteen points in the finals last season— young Red Blake, son of Ridgewood's leading book-maker.

Chapter 6

The first half was dying in a frenzy of noise and excitement as Central City, playing with desperation against the champs, cut the margin from eleven points to seven, and then to five. Yet all the while the crowd had the feeling that Ridgewood was under wraps and could run away with the game at any moment.

Just before the end of the half a foul was called. Groans and cries came from the Central City stands. Little Tom stepped to the line, bounced the ball twice, bent his knees, and tossed the first shot in. The referee grabbed the ball as it fell and handed it to him again. Again with that assurance of the tournament veteran, he bounced it on the floor, looked up, and flipped it coolly through the net.

Central City brought the ball out. Most of the crowd missed Tom's quick gesture as the ball came down and the pattern on the floor changed. He turned and flipped a kiss with his fingers toward a figure in a white skirt and white sweater on the side lines. If the crowd in the stands missed this, Mary Jo Berry didn't. Neither did Hooks Barnum sitting on the bench, his shoulders hunched over and a frown on his forehead.

The first half ended with the score 28-21 in Ridgewood's favor. In the second half, however, the Ridgewood B team found the going tough, and before the third quarter was over the varsity was sent back in again. Central City was a small school but their team was well coached, and when Tom took the floor again Ridgewood was leading by only four points. The varsity stood near the side lines, arms on each other's shoulders.

"Le's go, big team . . . let's ring this one up . . . le's get these guys."

They raced onto the floor, and as they did so the stands rose, cheering. Now the big boys are back. Now you'll really see something. Now, said everyone in the stands, they'll cut these kids down to size.

Tom got the ball almost immediately, glanced round mechanically for big Red, realized Red was no longer playing. Red, who guessed his fakes and feints, who could tell a step ahead just what he would do, was watching the game on television with his father in Mac and Joe's Bar and Grill. While the varsity was on the floor with Strings Johnson, the big six-foot-six colored giant, at center.

At times he slowed them up, almost held back their offense. Certainly he wasn't any Red Blake.

Tom faked deftly, dodged his defensive man, came down the floor, pivoted sharply. He flipped an overhead pass to the big boy standing there in the center, arms outstretched. But a hand reached out from nowhere and smacked at the ball, and with a feeling of annoyance Tom saw the Central City player slap it down and deflect it toward their goal. He reached it, grabbed it, and with a quick break was down the floor.

The pack thundered after him, the two Ridgewood guards closing in, Tom at his heels. But the little fellow was fast; he dodged past Ned, tore in for a lay-up, got it away safely. The ball tottered on the rim . . . and fell through.

A gigantic roar, a cry of sudden, piercing elation possessed the gymnasium. The place became a madhouse as the small Central City contingent in the stands realized victory was a possibility. On the electric scoreboard at the end the lights flashed, flickered, changed. Central City, 31; Ridgewood, 33.

They were now only two points ahead. We better snap out of this, and quick, thought Tom, as Harry brought the ball out, came down, and passed it to him. He eyed the court and his teammates, surveying the floor, slipped it to Ned, watched his teammates dart in and out followed by their guards. Then Tom

got the ball again, looked for an opening, and gave
a hand-off to Joe, who came back to Strings, who
returned it to Tom, who immediately slipped it
back to Strings, who pivoted and shot. The throw
was wide and a struggle ensued under the basket.

Then came that piercing yell again. Central City
had the ball.

Tom was not precisely upset or worried, but he
did not like things at all. He knew Strings should
not have shot then; he should have waited for a
good opening or a chance to get in. That big boy
was certainly not Red Blake by a long ways.

The figure in blue started down the floor. The
ball was across the ten-second line, going round the
circle, players cutting in and out, when suddenly
a Central City man dashed into the corner, turned,
jumped, and threw. Miraculously he hit the bucket.
Central City, 33; Ridgewood, 33.

Directly below was the time left: 3.34. Three
minutes and thirty-four seconds to go, and now it
was wide open. It was anyone's game to win.

Suspense hung over the packed bleachers. A fever
gripped the crowd. From the stands came cheers,
shouts, appeals, wild incoherent cries, as Tom, face
set, lips tight, took the ball in enemy territory.

Isn't this something! Ridgewood is in danger! The
big boys, the champs, the guys who slugged you

just by running out there in their red-and-white suits, were being held by a nobody.

Who was this giant killer? A township school with 350 students, and half that number from which to pick a team.

Tom knew what the trouble was. Now that Red was out they were a team no longer; they were no longer the smooth-working machine that had won sixteen straight games. They were four veterans attempting to assimilate a newcomer—work him into their style of play. He realized the danger, watched his teammates, their mouths open, trying feverishly to get in, to penetrate that tight defense, to score, anyhow—under the basket or over their heads—by any method and any means that would win the game and keep their record clean.

"Ah . . ." The stands rose together.

Big Strings Johnson, the new man, unable to stand the increasing pressure as the seconds ticked away, suddenly turned.

No, Strings, don't chuck it away, don't throw, thought Tom from across the floor, as he saw his teammate whirl toward the basket. Too late! The throw was hurried, so naturally it was high, far above the hoop. It looked like what it was—a wild, desperate stab in a tight spot.

The ball smacked the backboard, and Tom's heart sank as he saw it bounce directly into the arms of an opponent who had no business being where he was at the moment. He turned, feinted, passed to a teammate who raced wildly up the floor, while the yelling grew louder, and louder still. From man to man the ball went round, back and forth, cleanly handled. Tom realized now that these kids were not cracking. He saw with dismay that the pressure was not on Central City but on Ridgewood. It was a grim moment.

Then one small Central City player took the ball, pivoted, passed, took it back under the hoop and, flipping it back over his head, sank it for another basket.

Again that wild piercing shriek came, that noise which smothered the whole arena, which assaulted Tom's ears, beat at his brain.

Central City, 35; Ridgewood, 33. Two minutes and twenty-five seconds to go.

C'mon now, guys! C'mon, let's go, let's go, team! Let's show these fellas! Tom watched Joe take the ball out, quickly now as the fateful seconds ticked away. Tom took it from Joe, trying not to show the anxiety in his heart. He crossed the ten-second line and flipped the ball to Strings, who slipped it to Harry Greathouse, who broke loose and went in, and under . . .

There was a sudden sharp whistle. Somebody had fouled.

Tom saw Hooks Barnum rise from the bench protesting, take several steps along the floor, and stand there watching, tense, tight, unhappy.

The referee ran over and pointed at Joe Boyd. Central City would have two tries for the bucket.

Instantly the Central City stands jumped up, yelling wildly, cheering and shrieking at their team, while the Ridgewood cheering section booed and shouted.

"Central . . . Central . . . can't you see . . .
All you need is the referee."

The two squads sorted themselves out around the foul circle. Tom automatically smacked Joe on the shoulder, poked Harry's back, urging them to get going. He heard Joe mutter to nobody in particular, "That-there referee! He must be a Central City graduate. . . . I didn't foul him then."

"Yeah," said Tom, at his side. "He must be their principal. We'll get it back, kid, we will."

He glanced at the clock, miserable now, feeling the unfairness of it—asking them to play without Red, without their best man! If only Red was in there instead of that uncertain Strings Johnson, why, with Red beside him, nothing to it!

Harry, beside the circle, was hollering at the Central City man to upset him, and from the side lines Tom could hear the sharp, shrill cries of the

Davis twins on the bench. "Hi! Hi! Miss. You'll miss . . . miss . . ."

Trouble was, the Central City player hadn't been missing all evening. Nor did he begin at that critical moment, either. Without listening, without hearing the agonized shrieks all around, without seeing a thing save that hoop on the board above, he sank the first one, took the ball from the referee, bounced it calmly as if he were practicing on his own gym floor, and threw. The ball swished the net as it fell in. Central City, 37; Ridgewood, 33.

The dying seconds of the game ticked off. Usually at this point Ridgewood was freezing the ball and Tom, with a secure feeling, was watching their opponents fight vainly back, anguish in every heart and plain on every face. Now, for a change, it was Ridgewood who took the chances and threw the long, reckless shots, who became wild and careless. Now the crowd were on their feet, yelling at Tom, pleading, cheering, shifting glances from the floor to the clock. Twenty seconds. Nineteen seconds. Eighteen seconds . . .

Look! It's almost over! Can you believe it? We're beaten by this gang of kids, by this team from nowhere, from a district school.

Hey, look at Tom McWilliams go in. Watch him outjump that big center of theirs. He has it . . .

he's down now, feinting, ducking, passing the ball, taking it back, turning to shoot . . .

The ball fell through, and all Ridgewood shouted with joy. But only a few seconds remained. The great Redskins, the vets, the team that had swept the boards at Indianapolis the previous March, were dying on their own floor before their own crowd. Losing to a gang of kids from a district school which had been beaten by everyone in the county.

The tall Central City guard brought the ball out slowly, taking all the time he could, down past the ten-second line . . .

Bang! There it was. The game was over. It was official now. Ridgewood had lost!

A mighty shriek of joy rose, and the Central City contingent poured onto the floor, grabbing their tired and sweaty players, smacking their wet backs, their arms, any place they could reach, laughing, shouting, yelling.

Yeah, laugh, you guys, thought Tom, turning away, despair in his heart. It's all so unfair—to bust up a good team. Serves Barnum dead right we lost. You drop your best man, well, naturally . . .

At the end of the court, a Central City player was being hoisted up on a dozen shoulders to cut down the nets. "Here! Here's a knife!" "Hand it up to him!"

Slowly, dejectedly, Tom moved toward the dressing room, his head down. Somebody clung to his arm, and he looked down to find Mary Jo trying to console him. He shook her off roughly, disengaged himself, and vanished in the mob by the exit.

Get lost, guys, get lost!

Meanwhile, from the bench, Andy and Randy, the guards on the B team, paused for a moment to watch the fantastic scene. It hurt them as it did every Ridgewood player and fan to see the visitors celebrate. They felt in no hurry to go. The dressing room of a defeated team, especially one that has lost unexpectedly, is not a happy place. So the Davis twins stood watching. Now the nets were gone. In the milling mob on the floor, the Central City squad were surrounded by their delirious supporters.

"Ya know, Andy, know what? I believe we could have done better'n that out there tonight."

Chapter 7

In all his three years under Hooks Barnum, Little Tom could not recall ever having been asked before to report at the gym on a Saturday after a Friday night game. Passing through the corridor, he noticed half a dozen boys in their stocking feet on the floor shooting baskets, a gang from the eighth and ninth grades. Like everyone else, they had assumed the gym would be free that morning.

The varsity dressing room in the field house was a smallish room with windows high up on the wall, lockers around three sides, one door leading to the shower, another to the passage into the gymnasium. There were benches on the concrete floor in front of the steel lockers.

When Little Tom entered that day, he saw the whole squad sitting there in street clothes. "What's the idea?" he asked.

"Dunno. He just said for us not to get dressed; guess he doesn't want any practice this morning."

Then Hooks appeared, walking with his quick, nervous gait. Closing the door, he moved across to the table that supported the blackboard, a thickset, strong man of medium height with wide shoulders. There was a deep furrow above his eyes, and to Tom, who knew him well, that furrow seemed deeper than ever. He held a basketball, slapping it back and forth as he stood silently before them, looking at each one carefully.

Their heads were down, their eyes avoided his; they glanced at the floor, knowing what was to come.

"Well . . . anything you guys got to say? If you have, say it. You climbed into the driver's seat. You figgered you were safe because you had a lead of seven points at the half over those nobodies; because you were the great Redskins you thought they'd never dare catch you. Then when they did, you folded. Thought you'd get by the easy way, on your reputation. The champs! Ha! Won the State last year! You found out different; you got a bunch of gutsy kids that weren't scared of you for once, didn't you?"

Not a head rose; not a sound came from the benches. Tom was stung, yet he knew it was true and so did the others. They said nothing; what could they say?

"Now you realize a team can't get by on its reputation alone. At least that's something."

The ball slapped from hand to hand, back and forth, as he talked. The scorn in his tone burned them, hurt every boy in the room, even the B team players like Andy and Randy Davis, who had watched most of the game from the bench.

"Ran down that floor like you had boxcars attached to your shoes! Holding that ball, grandstanding out there, playing for a girl on the side lines. You know who I'm talking to! And you, Joe, you didn't make six good passes all evening. Harry, you let that little chap get inside you every time. Big shots! You found out different."

He saw me, thought Tom, he noticed me wave to Mary Jo. Gosh, I wish I hadn't . . . I wish we could play the game over. He shifted his weight and the bench creaked. Otherwise there was deep silence in the little room when the coach stopped talking. There he stood, glaring at Harry Greathouse and Little Tom and Joe and Ned Spencer—his veterans who had won the State—at Strings Johnson and the B team who had gone in, too.

Then with no warning he turned and snapped at Tom. "Did you go to that dance over to Rossville after the game last night?"

All the faces turned toward Tom. The benches

creaked. They all waited, watching to see whether he would come clean.

He choked, tried to say something, couldn't find his voice, and nodded miserably.

The coach didn't say a word. He merely stared hard at him, moving his head from side to side almost imperceptibly. Then he turned down the line of benches. "Harry, where were you yesterday afternoon?"

Another long silence. It hurt, yet it had to come. Gosh, thought Tom, the guy knows everything about everyone.

"Playing snooker, Hooks."

"At Mac and Joe's?"

The boy nodded. This was like being up before the principal, only worse, because Hooks knew his stuff. He didn't guess, he didn't speculate; he had the goods on you. He knew; he was tough.

"Joe, were you there too, by any chance? And how about you, Ned?"

There was another long silence. It seemed as if the boys would never reply. At last, heads down, they both mumbled, "Yeah, Hooks."

"Mighty glad you didn't lie to me. 'Cause I happen to know just where you were after school let out." The ball moved viciously from one palm to another. Slap-slap, slap-slap, the sound echoed through the room.

Tom twisted his cap nervously in his fingers, flipped back the ear tabs, stuffed it in his pocket. Nobody else stirred. The line up and down the benches was motionless.

Hooks continued. "Now you four boys all broke my training rules right after I specially warned you early in the week on this. Tom went to the Rossville dance. You three played snooker before a game; you walked a couple of miles round that table in that cigar smoke and took the edge off your condition. So we lost to a second-rate team because you didn't have it out there in the last quarter. Hope you learned a lesson. They're all tough in Indiana.

"I might have kept the B team in there; think mebbe they could have won. But I'd rather lose and have you learn things the hard way. You thought all you had to do was show on the floor and Central City would quit. Now if you want to go to dances and play pool, that's all right. But you *cannot play on any team I coach.*

"Get that straight. You all know my rules. There aren't many, but I expect you to keep 'em. That goes for the whole team, you four veterans and Strings and the B team, too. For Tom and Joe and Harry and Ned, same's everybody else. Dances are out. No pool or snooker. Stay away from the beer joints. Bed at ten unless I give you late permission.

This is the second time I'm warning you, and believe me it's the last time."

Slap-slap went the ball as it moved from one nervous hand to the other. He paused, looking at them. The heads along the row of benches were still down, jaws were motionless. Nobody glanced up as he continued.

"Now you four boys are going to play on the B team awhile. Andy and Randy and the others will take over. They'll play against Newcastle next week. Maybe they'll be in there the following week —I haven't made up my mind yet."

Heads came up quickly, an outraged, incredulous look on every face. Say! This is grim! Everybody in town will know what happened. The whole town will be asking questions. Folks will know we broke training.

Hi there, Tom! Didn't you play against Newcastle? You didn't? Going in against Marbletown this week, aren't you? Say, Joe, you playing the Marbletown game? I hear he had you on the B team all week. That right?

"But Hooks!" Tom's voice was thin and croaky, yet as a kind of unofficial spokesman he had to speak. "Two weeks from last night is the Marbletown game." Surely Hooks wouldn't risk playing the B team against Marbletown. Why, everyone knew he'd rather break a leg than lose to Marble-town.

The whole bench looked up, waiting expectantly. He had paid no attention to the suggestion. Instead he merely said, "That's all this morning. Practice Monday, same time as usual. I hope to see you make it good, too."

They wasted no time getting away. The benches sounded like firecrackers as they scraped against the concrete floor. Usually when they poured out of the room there were shouts and lusty cries. Now they went out silently, without a word. Their faces told how they felt. Caps in their hands, the Redskins, the champs, the men who had beaten the best at Indianapolis the previous March, shuffled quickly and quietly into the hall. They couldn't get away from that room fast enough.

Chapter 8

Had it been summer, the two of them would have been sitting together on the vine-covered porch; but as it was December, they were in the Berrys' living room on the big couch before the television set. The television was off. Television didn't interest either one that night.

Little Tom felt as unhappy as he ever had, for years. His world seemed united against him, even Mary Jo, who should have been on his side and usually was. They sat close as they always did, yet that evening they were miles apart.

"What did your father say?"

"My old man! He's the mayor; he doesn't like Sam Blake. Besides, he's just the same as the rest of the older people. Can't you understand, Mary Jo? Red didn't do anything that everyone else in town doesn't do."

"What he did is to show kids in high school how to gamble, to teach them to bet. He kept a book,

he got kids into betting. I should think you'd
realize . . ."

"But that isn't immoral. Everyone in town bets.
Your old man, my old man, everybody. There's
even slot machines in the locker room of the country
club."

"No! How'd you find that out?"

"I saw them. I often have to go get Dad in the
car after his golf. I've seen those men playing the
machines. There's slot machines in the Elks' club-
house and the Legion's, and don't think the police
department doesn't know it, either. Who do they
think they're fooling with all this talk about gambling? Red makes a friendly little book on the fight.
Then what? They jump on him and chuck him out
of school, and we'll lose the State. It's unfair; it's
not right. Even Hooks Barnum—I always thought
he saw our angle; now he talks like a preacher."

She put her hand on his big fist and sighed.
"Look, Tom. Look at it this way. Old Hitchcock
had to do it; he couldn't do anything else. Suppose
a kid was asked what he learned in school and
answered, 'Why, I learned how to make a book on
the fights.' See what I mean?"

"That's a foolish answer to a foolish question."

"But don't you understand?"

"No, I don't. All I see is, everyone's against us.
Even you are. Even Hooks Barnum. Hooks was a

right guy until we won the State for him; now look at him. D'you know what? He threatens not to let us fellas on the varsity play against Marbletown. We're gonna play, though."

She looked at him quickly. "How d'you mean you're gonna play?"

"Why, what I mean is, we've talked it over, the four of us, and we know what we're doing. If he doesn't use us against Marbletown a week from Friday, we'll quit the squad, that's all. Maybe that'll show him," he said bitterly.

"Oh . . . Tom," she said, as he rose, reaching for his cap and coat. At last he had made an impression. She stood and put her hands up on his shoulders. "Don't do anything in a hurry, Tom; don't put him on a spot. He's upset and sore over things, just like you are."

"Humph! If he is, he sure doesn't show it. He won't do anything about Red."

"Oh, but I know he is. I noticed him in the cafeteria yesterday; he looks five years older than he did a month ago. This is hard for him. He has a family, remember that. Folks forget a coach wants to win as much as anybody. Why, last year you all loved him."

He glanced down at her as she pleaded. Last year I did love him, he thought, that's right; now he's against me. He and my father and the principal and even you are against me.

Tom was sore and hurt and angry. What he wanted at that moment was to hurt someone else and if it was someone he loved, all the better. "Yeah, we did; but he's changed. He's not the same Hooks Barnum he was. Besides, this doesn't depend on me only, it depends on the other guys. We'll call Hooks. We'll make him play us. Well . . . I must get along." He went toward the front door. "Good night, Mary Jo."

She turned away so he wouldn't see her tears. "Good night, Tom."

When Hooks Barnum came into the dressing room that next afternoon, he saw immediately what the principal or some casual observer might have missed. The B team were sitting on the benches dressed to play, or they were getting dressed. But the veterans, the varsity, the backbone of the squad, were sitting in front of their lockers in their street clothes. They hadn't even taken off their shoes.

Little Tom knew by Hooks' raised eyebrows as he came in that he had sized up the situation, so before the coach could speak he rose. His seventy-six inches towered over everything and everyone in the room. All movements ceased as he stood. Coondog Smith, the stocky colored boy, a forward on the B team, paused in the act of lacing a shoe. Randy Davis, struggling into his pants, hesitated.

"Hooks . . ." said Tom in a shaky tone, while every face turned toward him, "we . . ."

"Who's we?"

It bothered Tom, threw him off stride, off the track of his prepared and carefully rehearsed speech on which they had all spent so much time.

"Why . . . now . . . er . . . we . . . we fellows, us guys on the varsity who played last year . . ."

"Oh! I see. Just wanted to be sure who you were speaking for." Hooks certainly wasn't making things easy. Perhaps he had guessed what was coming. Strikes had happened before in Indiana basketball. Jack Morgan had had to face one at South Bend, and Briggs Rider at Gary, and that man at Tech last year. All this was part of basketball history, and every seventh-grader in the state knew it.

"Yessir, yes, Hooks . . . now, we . . . I mean . . . you said Saturday that the B team would play this week against Newcastle. That right?"

"I said the boys who broke my training rules were off the varsity temporarily. I cannot have boys on the team who don't care enough to keep training. You smoke, you go out nights, you break rules—you take the consequences. The B team will play the Newcastle game. That's all set."

"Yes . . . uh-huh . . . Hooks, we understand, we

appreciate that. Then you said, Saturday morning, that you hadn't quite made up your mind about who you'd play the next week end."

"That's correct."

"But that's the week end of the Marbletown game."

The second Tom uttered the magic word, heads went up. Every face in the row of benches was turned toward him. To be sure, it was only an early-season match; it wasn't in a tournament. Nothing was at stake except the win-and-lose record, a record that had already been damaged by Central City. However, this would be Ridgewood against Marbletown.

Beat Marbletown! Every merchant in town, every farmer in the county, every man, woman, and child in Ridgewood would rather beat Marbletown than any other team on the schedule. And would rather lose to anyone else, too.

Naturally, Tom realized, if you were in your right mind you wouldn't yank six-foot-four veterans of the State and put in the B team with players like the Davis twins, Andy and Randy, the five-foot-eight guards. Sure those kids are speed merchants, sure they are, but they can't go up after the rebounds like we can.

So they had Hooks cold. He would have to let

them play against Marbletown. Of course, maybe he intended to, only they wanted to make sure.

"Yes," Hooks answered reflectively. "H'm, yes, the Marbletown game." As if he'd forgotten the existence of Marbletown.

"We just wanted to know . . . to be sure . . . about Marbletown. You said you hadn't hardly decided on your line-up for a week from Friday."

"I know I did. I hadn't decided, either."

Tom noticed his puzzled face, watched the furrow deepen over his eyes. Mary Jo was right; he looked much older. Now he was up against it. For Hooks always liked to pretend that he was more than a coach, that he worked with all the boys, not the varsity only, but the B team and the subs as well. At least, so he said in speeches in assembly and at the Kiwanis dinner downtown. He believed that what counted was this test of character. Somebody had to lose and somebody had to win. The important thing was meeting fate head on.

Now fate was meeting him head on. Maybe this would be a lesson to him, maybe now he would do something about Red's troubles. He'd better; folks like to win in Ridgewood. That's basketball in Indiana.

Hooks stood quietly before them and Little Tom saw he was trapped. "The Marbletown game," he said at last. "Nope, I hadn't forgotten about the

Marbletown game. I told you last Saturday my mind wasn't completely made up about the line-up for that game. Well, I've just decided on it. You fellas have helped me come to a decision."

Heads went up quickly around the room. Tom saw the tension ease on the crowded benches. He glanced at Harry, who winked back ever so slightly, and at Joe, whose lips smiled. Yep, they had him. No coach could expect to beat Marbletown with little runts like the Davis twins in there. Of course not.

"Yes, I've made up my mind. Same line-up as against Newcastle this week."

Every boy in the room was stunned. Tom felt suddenly cold all over. Harry's jaw dropped; the smile quickly left Joe's lips. Ned shifted his feet. Even the subs were staggered. Strings Johnson, the big colored giant leaning lazily against his locker, glanced up with apprehension on his face.

Dismayed, upset, the roomful of boys looked at the coach. Why, he's crazy! We can't ever beat Marbletown with the twins and Coondog and Shorty and Strings. He's gone mad! They glanced at each other, really alarmed now, their feelings reflected on their faces.

Why, the guy's double-crossed us!

Little Tom stood there awkwardly. A moment before he was on top; he had the guy where he

wanted him. Now, as their spokesman, he hardly
knew what to say. He hated to go through with it,
but they had agreed, all four of them, so there was
nothing else to do.

"Hooks . . . well . . . now . . . we feel . . .
the varsity . . . us vets, that is . . . we feel you
aren't being fair about this. Two weeks is too long
a suspension, we feel. We understand about Newcastle, but if we can't play against Marbletown next
week . . . well . . ."

Here it comes. Hold on to your seats, fellas. We
agreed, remember. We gotta stick together; you
told me to say it.

"If we can't play against Marbletown, we'd just
rather not play at all."

Now they had him cold. This would show him.
After all, they were the veterans, the Redskins who
had won the State and been given P-rades and
banquets and celebrations and presented with gold
wrist watches and things. They had sat on the stage
at assembly and heard everyone talk about them and
tell what great guys they were. A wonderful bunch
. . . fine boys . . . all of them . . . not merely a
good basketball team, but a credit to the city of
Ridgewood, a swell crowd to work with, to fight
through the State with.

All this they had heard and heard many times
—from the school authorities, from Rotary and

Kiwanis. They had read it in the papers, too. You mightn't, of course, believe the *Sentinel*. But if Bill Fox says so in his column in the Indianapolis *News*, then it must be so, mustn't it?

Outside in the corridor they heard the slap-slap, slap-slap of balls on the concrete floor as some younger kids ran past the room onto the gym floor. A car roared by on the street. Nobody spoke. Everyone was thinking hard, especially the veterans. Say, how did we get into this spot? Why, the guy has crossed us up!

At that moment the door opened and Mr. Collier, the dean, poked his face inside, his spectacles glittering in the beam of sunshine from the window in the wall above. He took one look at the coach, at Little Tom standing uneasily before him, at the serious faces of the boys on the benches. "Oh! Excuse . . . excuse me." He closed the door as gently as if he had been interrupting a prayer meeting. They might have snickered had it been just an ordinary blackboard session. This was far too grim. This was basketball history.

Hooks spoke as the door closed. "You'd prefer not to be considered for the varsity any more, that right?"

Little Tom nodded.

"You really mean that, Tom? You really know

what you're saying? Have you thought this thing
through? Have you, you fellas?"

"Yessir, we voted on it. We had a meeting at
Harry's house yesterday. If we can't play against
Marbletown, we really don't care to play any more.
That goes for all four of us." He turned. "Hey,
fellas?"

"Yeah."

"Yep, that's right."

Their voices were not very certain. The fact was
they had not anticipated that he would cross them
up. Yet their heads bobbed assent.

However, Hooks persisted, trying to find a way
out, to break them down. "You certain about this,
Harry?"

Tom remembered how Harry had run to the
bench the moment the gun sounded that night at
Indianapolis and kissed Hooks, how Joe had come
after him. And how he himself had insisted that
Hooks climb the stepladder there in the field house
and cut down his share of the net.

"Joe, you really want to go through with this?
Ned Spencer . . . you . . ."

His tone of appeal hit them, every one, because
they had all been through so much the previous year
together. But at the moment they were sore. They
forgot the closeness of their association. All they
remembered was the unjustness of Red's dismissal

from school, their own punishment for breaking training, plus the fact that this was the Marbletown game they were talking about. This gang had never lost to Marbletown. They also knew Hooks wanted to beat Marbletown more than any other team on the schedule.

Tom remembered with regret his confident remark when the four of them had met the previous day. "Look, if he doesn't play us, this town will take him apart. That's for certain." Because Ridgewood had tasted victory. Once you've tasted it you want more.

Hooks stood looking at them. Finally his chin rose and he spoke with a firm tone. "Right. If that's how you four feel, I've nothing more to say. If you want to go ahead with this thing, well, it's up to you. Strings!"

The tall colored boy leaning against his locker heard his name and almost tumbled off the bench. Any other time the crowd would have laughed, and that would have helped.

"Strings! You'll take over at center definitely from now on. Coondog, you go in for Tom. Andy and Randy, the guards. Shorty, you take over Harry's spot." Hooks looked around the room a minute and then said suddenly, brutally, "And get moving! I've got too many standing ballplayers."

Tom knew what he meant. His head buzzed. Well, this is it. The guy's double-crossed us. Now we've done it, we've cut clean. He heard the familiar words, the words he himself had so often used.

"All right, gang, let's go!"

"Let's go, big team . . . let's go!"

Not today, not that afternoon, the big team wasn't going. One member of the big team was playing blackjack on a beer-stained table in Mac and Joe's Bar and Grill on Indiana Avenue. The rest of the big team were sitting there in front of their lockers, dressed in slacks and windbreakers, twiddling their caps in their fingers, stunned and bewildered. They were the veterans. They were through.

The B team rose hesitantly, uncertain about their new role, worried and unhappy. Now it's up to us. Now we have to face Marbletown. Gee . . .

They moved toward the door, basketballs in their hands.

"Let's go, gang . . . let's go!"

It sounded feeble. There was no health in it.

Chapter 9

In the state of Indiana, it isn't the high-school team or the kids' team; it's Ridgewood, Bedford, Lafayette, Hammond, Franklin, or Martinsville. The team belongs to the whole town. Consequently, when anything affects the team it affects everyone in town.

It took only about twenty minutes for Slim Harris, the sports editor of the Ridgewood *Sentinel*, to get to the gym that afternoon to check on the rumor he had heard. He was closely followed by Stanley Watters, the radio announcer of Station WRLK. Hooks Barnum was on the floor with the B team, and a glance told both men the rumor was true.

Uptown, around town, the news spread, into homes, stores, factories, into the big Chrysler plant just as the day shift came off, into the office of the principal, who immediately telephoned the news to the superintendent of schools. Serious business, this tampering with a winning team in Ridgewood.

Others found it out when the boys on the varsity appeared around town instead of staying for practice. Most concerned was Sam Blake in Mac and Joe's Bar and Grill, to whom this meant money. Telephones jangled in business offices as the afternoon wore on. By nightfall the whole town knew what had taken place and everyone was discussing it.

"D'ja hear what Barnum did with his first team?"

"Say, I understand Barnum has fired his whole doggone varsity."

"What on earth is this Barnum trying to do, anyhow—lose the State?"

After all, things looked bad for the Newcastle game, because you can't throw an inexperienced team against a bunch of vets and expect to win. As for Marbletown the next week, it would be a slaughter with midgets like Andy and Randy Davis in the line-up.

The Davis twins were well known in Ridgewood and not because their father was the town's leading druggist, either. In the first place, they were top scorers on the B team, which hadn't lost a game in two seasons. Fast, dependable, they were the cutters, the dribble masters, the scooters of the squad. But it was not for basketball they were celebrated. They were pranksters. If there was trouble at Halloween, folks knew the Davis twins were responsible. At the big bonfire for the varsity after the State, one of them ran the fire chief's car into a vacant lot behind the high school, and hours passed before it was discovered. They especially enjoyed switching newpapers on the afternoon paper routes, exchanging *Sentinels* for copies of the *News*. You could be sure if any mischief took place in town, the twins were behind it.

Only during basketball season, when they were busy, did they behave. With Strings Johnson, Shorty McCall, and Coondog Smith, they had made up the B team, tough in its class. Coondog, five ten, with sturdy legs, strong thighs, and a thick torso, was the star of the varsity football team. His quick reflexes made him a dangerous competitor in any sport. But four of these men were under six feet and Strings, the jumping center, had trouble getting up on the backboards. Now they were replacing the famous Redskins, winners of the State the previous March.

Naturally the idea shocked all Ridgewood. Folks assaulted Hooks Barnum everywhere, pestered him at the Kiwanis luncheons, ganged up on him when he got his hair cut or ventured downtown after practice. At home his telephone jangled incessantly. To everyone he gave the same answer. One man had been expelled by the principal for gambling.

The other four members of the varsity had not kept training, so he had demoted them for a couple of weeks. They had all felt this was unfair and decided that if they couldn't play against Marbletown they wouldn't continue on the squad. They made the decision; he accepted it. What else could he do?

This always brought the same reaction, a kind of confused, bewildered splutter. "Yes, sure, yeah; but after all, you can't expect to beat Marbletown with a couple of clowns like the Davis kids and that big, lazy colored boy, that Strings Johnson."

Hooks quietly agreed. "We probably won't beat Marbletown."

Folks looked hard at him and walked on. "Say! What on earth has happened to Barnum? He must be clean out of his senses to break up a veteran team that won the State and go with those Davis twins."

"Seems to me he's crazy, putting in Johnson. Why, that boy used to have trouble getting down under Coondog's passes all last fall, remember?"

These were not the only things said after the Newcastle game. For the team played below themselves. They were all frightened at being the center of so much controversy. One day they were the B team and tops in their own class. Next day they were out on the floor as the Ridgewood varsity. So, after holding the Trojans pretty well at first, ending the half only a few points down, they broke in the third quarter. The Newcastle forwards began getting in under the basket, and when they didn't actually score were often fouled in the act of shooting.

Immediately, of course, the Redskins lost their heads; they started shooting from way out and missing. The score mounted. When the gun sounded, Ridgewood had lost, 68-41. It was almost the worst defeat the team had suffered since Hooks Barnum came to town. The B team had been plenty tough in its own class. When overnight it became the varsity, it was in a different and harder league.

This defeat, which Little Tom and Red Blake watched from high up in the stands, was not too difficult for them to take. They agreed it served Hooks right—the guy had it coming to him—and as they walked home after the game both felt sure that after a few more such contests the town would have a new coach. Then they would both be back in there playing for Ridgewood again.

What was hard, however, was the void in Tom's life. Each afternoon now was a thousand hours long and, worse still, it was purposeless. He began to dread the sound of the last bell, because it meant an eternity until dinner with nothing to do. Since Mary Jo felt Hooks was right, he had no wish to see her, and evenings were just as bad. At last he fell back upon his homework merely to keep busy.

As he expected, he got little sympathy from his father, who seemed not to care about a winning team. Once when Little Tom commented bitterly on the injustice of Hook Barnum's action, his father merely shook the *Sentinel*, and said impatiently, "I sorta wondered how long it would take Barnum to catch up with you fellas. Maybe you were just too big for your boots."

On the Monday after the Newcastle game, Red Blake was waiting for Tom around the corner when school let out and proposed they sneak up into the gym and watch Barnum take the new varsity apart. Up back of the scoreboard was a place where nobody could see them, so they went through the boiler room and up the back stairs, and hid themselves away in keen anticipation of what was to come. They knew from experience that Hooks Barnum was always tough on players who made mistakes, especially when they were repeated. Now those kids were in for it and their listless actions on the floor seemed to indicate that the business of being the first string wasn't as much fun as they had anticipated.

Hooks walked briskly out, dressed as usual in slacks, sweat shirt, and basketball shoes, a whistle on a cord around his neck. When he appeared, Red nudged Tom and grinned at him. Tom grinned back, and it was his first smile for some time, too.

The coach's whistle as he came onto the floor had
an ominous sound. The boys immediately left the
baskets at which they were shooting and formed
a circle around him: Andy and Randy, Coondog
Smith, Strings Johnson, Shorty McCall, and the
subs, who were mostly sophomores with little or no
experience.

Hooks' first words, which came clearly up to
them, astonished Red and Tom. "Now, fellas, let's
all forget that Newcastle game. It's behind us; forget
it. I've seen you play better ball—when you beat the
Anderson B team and when you beat the Wildcats
early last month. The Newcastle game is over. We
have work, lots of hard work ahead, and you'll all
have to work harder than you ever did before. I'll
work with you, too."

Tom noticed the heads around the circle come up
slowly. He wasn't chewing them up after all!

"Now one thing I want everyone to get. Each
boy on this floor . . . has a chance . . . to make . . .
the varsity. Regardless of his experience or lack of
it. This thing is wide open.

"We got a pasting Friday night. I expected that;
I wasn't surprised. There were one or two good
things about that game, though. You played like a
team at times; you held pretty well the first half.
Toward the end, no, you blew it; you were just
heaving that ball at the basket. Andy, you know

anyone can make a basket if he gets the ball at the right moment. That's team play. The man who feeds the ball, who passes at the exact second—he's the one who counts. He's my boy."

Tom noticed the circle stir restlessly, watching each movement he made, listening to every word he spoke. Somebody bounced a ball nervously, but Hooks didn't get on him as he had on Red a short time before. And the terrible dressing down both boys expected the B team to get after that defeat did not come.

Instead he said, "Every day from now on we'll all drill first on our passes. I don't go in much for bounce passes; you know that—a straight pass is better. In passing it's the timing and accuracy that count. Randy! Hit Strings in the belly with your pass. You too, Coondog. We must get our passes so you can throw with your eyes shut and hit your man every time.

"Basketball is a game of movement. Move and pass, move and pass. Andy, you and Randy were feinting and faking real good that first half; I was pleased. Then what happened? You were only five points back, and all at once the roof fell in. You just were not passing, you lost your heads, all of you. Move and pass, move and pass.

"Now, guys, let's face it. We're at the bottom. O.K., so we're at the bottom, and we'll get out if we all work harder than we ever worked before. And if we're at the bottom, there's only one way to go; that's up. Let's pull together, let's work together, every man."

They turned away, shouting, and there was meaning in their tones now. "Let's go . . . big team . . . let's go."

Tom and Red climbed down, shinnied over the rafters, and went out the back way without being seen by a soul. They were completely mystified.

"Nuts," said Red, "he'd have taken us apart for that, he would." His voice was bitter.

"Right, he would. He didn't eat them up, or laugh at them the way the *Sentinel* did today. He didn't blame them, or anything."

"I don't understand him," said Red.

"Me neither. Figure if that hadda been us out there this afternoon."

"Yeah, figure. 'Don't bounce that ball, Red. When I say quiet . . . I mean quiet.'" His voice wasn't a bad imitation of the coach's, either.

Chapter 10

Everyone was against Little Tom. His world had turned sour. Nobody seemed willing or able to feel the injustice that had been done except the other boys on the former varsity and a few friends. Not all his friends, by any means; some of them refused to stand up and be counted, for the school was bitterly divided on the issue. The principal was against him, of course; yes, naturally. He never could see a fellow's point of view. So was the dean; yes, he would be. But why was his father so blind, so stubborn, so unreasonable?

What hurt Tom even more was to be on the opposite side from Hooks, with whom he had been so close for so long. Of course Mary Jo's refusal to stick with him upset him most of all.

The trouble was, you couldn't do a single thing. You were licked, helpless, forced to sit up there in Seat 3, Row GG of the field house and watch those clumsy cowboys get trampled on by every second-rate team on the schedule. Wearing our uniforms, too, carrying our numbers, calling themselves the Redskins. No wonder Slim Harris in the *Sentinel* made fun of them. There was a smart newspaperman; he knew his way around. He saw the whole issue in a second; he understood, at least.

Then overnight, suddenly and without any warning, Tom found some people who did care, who understood and sympathized. That endless void, those long, everlasting afternoons with nothing whatever to do were no more. Overnight, he found himself plunged into an activity as full of effort and as demanding as the hours formerly spent in the school gymnasium.

The downtown pool on Ridgewood to reach the finals of the State had hit $12,000, a significant sum, and it was obvious that the men who had placed the cash would not lose it without a fight. They talked of having the first team reinstated by bringing pressure to bear politically and, if that didn't work, they would get Barnum's scalp somehow.

An informal meeting in Mac and Joe's was presided over by Sam Blake, who had a slice of cash in the pool himself, and half a dozen of the biggest betters were present. Little Tom sat on a table in the back of the room beside Red, really encouraged. The doors were shut and locked; he could see these men meant business.

After considerable discussion it was decided to start a petition for a new coach and get it signed by everyone in town. "We'll present it to the mayor for action," one man suggested.

Everyone's eyes turned toward Tom. He felt uncomfortable and a little ashamed of his father's position. Nevertheless he had to speak up. "Naw, Dad won't do a thing. He'll chuck any petition into the wastebasket; he thinks Hooks did just right."

There was an embarrassed silence, for this was news to most of those present.

Finally a man cleared his throat. "Yes," he said, "I've talked to Big Tom. As far as I can tell, the boy's dead right. It seems to me that we're just wasting time with the mayor; we should present the petition straight to the council and have them go after the school board. They will, too; they're really hot about this."

"I know Ray Means. He'd better do something."

"I know Jerry Smith. He feels the same as we do."

So the council was in the bag. Once an impressive number of signatures were collected and the petition calling on Hooks to resign was presented, he would have to go. Then they could pay his salary for the year, get in a new man as coach, reinstate the varsity, and go to town.

But first came the collection of signatures. For this the men were divided into teams, as for a Red

Cross drive. Little Tom was made captain of a group of school kids and told to handle the high school. This was not easy, for many of his pals refused to sign. However, at the urging of some of the men who realized his importance, he was sent out afternoons getting names in town.

This worked out well for everyone. The betting crowd were delighted to have the son of the mayor and a prominent member of the former varsity working for them. Tom was happy to be busy and doing something to correct the injustice under which he still smarted. But it was work, hard work. Lots of kids turned away when he approached them, and this hurt. Yet on the whole he liked it; everybody knew him, and downtown folks were eager to sign the petition. Once organized, the thing really got moving. Placards, *Sign the Petition*, appeared in the shop windows, in the stores along Walnut and Second Avenues, in the automobile salesrooms, the chain stores, the grills and pool parlors, even in the banks. Only a few places such as the Davis drugstore were without one.

After the Marbletown game, a 64-40 slaughter, about the worst Ridgewood ever had received from the Bearcats, the petition really picked up steam. Within forty-eight hours of the Marbletown defeat lots of prominent citizens had signed as a civic duty.

"Have you signed the petition?" everyone asked

everyone else. By being on the inside, Tom soon discovered that nearly every adult in town who counted had signed. It was a mass movement that swung people along like the excitement of an overtime game.

Drawn up by Lawyer Crane, the petition was a truly formidable document, full of pompous phrases. "Whereas we, the citizens of Ridgewood, Indiana, do have a particular pride and interest in our high-school basketball team . . ." and so on, for a dozen pages. The whole thing, boiled down, was a request to the school board to ask Hooks to reinstate his former varsity or resign.

One afternoon a week later Tom sauntered down Indiana Avenue, his duties done, reading with pleasure a headline on one of the sports pages of the *Sentinel:* "Barnum's Midgets Trimmed by Lafayette."

That's good—Barnum's Midgets. That's pretty good for Slim Harris. That's what they really are, a bunch of midgets.

Tom decided to run up to the gymnasium and clean out his locker, where he had left a lot of personal belongings, including some clippings and other things he wanted.

In the rear, where nobody could see him in the shadows, he stood beside the door of the gymnasium, the familiar sounds coming to him with a sharpness that hurt. That pound-pound of feet on the floor, those quick, shrill cries should have been his and Red's and Harry's, not those midgets' out there. He felt more resentful and angry at Hooks than ever. As he watched there was the accustomed piercing whistle. Play stopped and he heard the coach's voice.

"Strings! Look, boy, catch that ball. Catch it up there; you know how. Go up after it, as high as you can. Don't tip it in; I don't want a tipping team. Climb up on those backboards; get those bricks outa your britches. Let me see you jump, man, jump. You can do it; you got the height. Andy . . . Randy . . . How many times do I have to tell you to watch your passes? You're fast, you're smart; make those passes count."

Tom turned away. He hadn't seen much but he was satisfied. They'll never amount to anything; they're just five individuals all trying to get that ball into the bucket, each regardless of the other. You can't make kids like the Davis twins realize that a fast break and a quick dribble down the floor may look hot from the stands but don't spell teamwork. You can't build a forward line out of Coondog Smith and that McCall boy. And take Strings Johnson. Six feet six—he ought to be all-state, that boy. Only he's too lazy to move.

Tom collected his gear, stepped back into the hall, climbed up high in the stands where nobody could see him, and watched the ragged practice through to the end. At last the team tramped off the floor, followed by Hooks and his assistant, moving to the lockers. Tom came down, paused at the water cooler in a recess near the coach's room and, as he did so, heard a familiar voice.

"Had your vitamin pills yet today, fella?"

"Nosir. Not yet." It was Strings Johnson.

Tom bent over the drinking fountain, his clothes in a bundle under one arm.

"Be sure and get 'em. You rate 'em now you're on the varsity. Strings, where do you live, anyhow?"

Tom expected him to say Whistleville, where most of the colored people lived. Instead, he answered, "Out on the National Road. We have a farm out there."

In Ridgewood, Route 40, the cross-country highway which starts at the Atlantic Ocean and bisects the nation from there to San Francisco, is called the National Road. It cuts Indiana in two.

"How far out?"

"'Bout six miles. Then it's a mile and a half back from the highway."

"How do you get to school mornings? Take the bus?"

The boy must have nodded, for the coach continued, while Tom stood unable to move. "At night, after practice, when the bus is gone, what d'you do then?" This was the question Tom also wondered about and he waited with interest for the answer.

"Why, in the fall after football I could usually get me a ride. Now it's dark, folks won't pick up hitchers any more, so I just walk home."

Tom was staggered. That meant three hours or more of hard practice, then a six-mile walk along a concrete highway plus a mile and a half on a dirt road in the darkness. No wonder he wasn't much good up on those backboards.

"Strings, what's your father do?"

"Works in the Chrysler plant."

"Got any brothers or sisters?"

"Yessir, two brothers and a sister. Then there's my aunt's kids, her that was killed in the accident at Pride's Crossing two years ago."

"That so? How many youngsters out on that farm in all?"

"Eight."

"I see. Strings, what's your father make at Chrysler? They pay pretty good, don't they?"

"Well, his take-home pay is $57.50."

Tom did some quick figuring as he stood by the water fountain. Fuel. Clothes. Gas for the car. Food for ten people. Maybe they had some chickens and a few pigs and put up vegetables every summer. But he knew enough to realize it couldn't be easy.

"What did you eat this noon for lunch, Strings?"

"Why, I had me a sandwich and a bottle of milk."

Tom was shocked. He knew a sandwich and a bottle of milk didn't stay by you after three hours on that floor. So that was why Strings always ate off alone in the cafeteria, why he kept to himself.

"Did you buy that lunch in the cafeteria?"

"Nosir. My mother puts up sandwiches for us kids that comes in on the bus each morning."

Tom heard someone coming and started to move away. He just caught Hooks' last words.

"Tell you what, Strings. I want you to come downtown and have dinner with me this evening. Later on I'll run you out home."

His clothes bundled under one arm, Tom ducked out the side door, confused and bewildered. This was the old Hooks, the man who instinctively knew when kids were in trouble and who invariably had the answers, too.

His affection for the coach flared up inside him. For a moment the petition was far away; he was sitting on the bench at the finals, with Hooks' arm around his shoulders and Hooks' voice in his ears.

"Get in there, Tom boy, get in there and pull those kids together."

Only he wasn't in the field house at Indianapolis; he was walking down the path from the school steps, no longer a member of the varsity. Nearing the curb, he noticed a gang of boys standing around a familiar black sedan. They greeted him, but all eyes were upon the car, which he recognized as Hooks'.

Someone had slashed all four tires, and the automobile was sitting forlornly on its rims.

Tom was shocked. "Gee! Who did it? Who did that, fellas?"

They shrugged their shoulders. No one answered.

Chapter 11

In the wave of publicity that followed the transformation of the B team into the Ridgewood varsity, the name *Barnum's Midgets* swept up and down the state, getting laughs everywhere. Actually this was unfair, because Strings Johnson, the big center, was six feet six. However, the others were small for an Indiana basketball team, Shorty McCall, one of the forwards, being the tallest at five eleven.

When Ridgewood managed to win their first game, against Marion, just before the holidays, the *Sentinel* headline read, "Barnum's Midgets Win at Last."

It was plain that the team had become a pleasant sort of joke in sporting circles whenever basketball was mentioned.

The evening after the Marion game, Little Tom glanced up with surprise when his father tossed aside the afternoon newspaper with an angry gesture. "That man Hessler! What does he know about basketball?"

Tom, who never read anything but the comics and the sports pages, grabbed the paper. He was aware that Mr. Hessler had signed the petition, but he had hardly expected the front-page editorial, which was headed, "Barnum Should Resign."

It called on Hooks to reinstate his first team immediately and drill them for the coming Frankfort game or else give way to a new coach. A comfortable, warming sensation came over Little Tom as he read down the page. For Mr. Hessler swung his weight in town. Besides owning the *Sentinel* and Station WRLK, he was mixed up in about every enterprise in town. He was a director of two banks, president of the Chamber of Commerce and, generally speaking, Ridgewood's most important citizen. When he talked folks listened.

The mayor stood before the fireplace, filling his pipe with an annoyed gesture. Just then the telephone rang. "Tell 'em I'm not in, Mother. Just take the name. It's been ring-ring-ring all this week, at home and at the office. I haven't had a minute's peace with this basketball. The wolves are after me. They'd better save their breath. Let the wolves howl."

"They're after Barnum. That's who they're after. Dad, when the wolves howl in this town, you better watch your step. The school is against him, Dad, and the whole city is too. Ridgewood wants a winner."

"Right, my boy; you're right. And they don't care how they get one, either. Let me tell you something. That petition you're working on—oh, I've heard all about it—that won't do any good. The school board won't act, and this Barnum is tough; they won't scare him any. He has a contract until the end of the school year. What's more, I hope he doesn't quit under fire, either."

Tom refused to argue the point. He felt sure Hooks would be forced to resign by the determined group of men downtown. For he was seeing things from the inside now and knew more about the situation than his father. But he had to admit to himself that he was shaken the next morning to hear that Block R, the girls' cheering section, was planning a pep rally at practice that afternoon. Now why should they do that, he wondered. Why should they?

When he saw Mary Jo in the corridor between classes he went up to her, although they had not spoken for a fortnight. "Some girls in our home room say Block R is giving a pep rally at practice this afternoon."

She looked up at him with her big eyes and tossed her hair back. "What of it?"

"I only wanted to know, that's all. Seems kinda

funny you never gave us guys a pep rally in practice."

She faced him squarely. "You didn't need it."

"Yeah, maybe. Only this gang hasn't done anything to deserve it, you must admit that. Unless you call beating Marion something. Gee, everyone in the county has trimmed Marion. You never gave us a pep rally."

"Look, Tom McWilliams, we gave you support, plenty." She tossed her hair again. "This team needs encouragement right now; it's up to the school to give it to them."

"But, Mary Jo, you know Hooks is going to resign soon."

"Who . . . why . . . He is? How d'you know?"

"Oh, I'm on the inside—I know what's going on downtown; I have means of finding things out. You saw the editorial in last night's *Sentinel*, didn't you? Well, the town won't take it much longer; the town won't stand for him. Please call this thing off, please . . ."

"No. We want to back the team. They're our team. We'll go through with it."

By this time he was angry. "They are *not* your team, those midgets. *We're* the team, the varsity, the real team. We'll be back in there, too."

"You? You guys are just a bunch of soreheads."

He was completely surprised and upset. "Who?

Me? Us guys?" The idea amazed him. It was a new idea; nobody had suggested anything of the sort. Of course not! It was untrue, completely untrue.

They stood there silently until a teacher approached them. "The bell has rung, Tom," she said.

He turned and went bitterly to his class, thinking how close they had been and how long they had known each other. During the years when he had climbed slowly to the subs and then the B team and finally the varsity, Mary Jo was working her way up to become one of the yell leaders. In the state of Indiana it is almost as hard to be a high-school yell leader as to be a forward on the basketball team.

She began her practicing sophomore year, and after tryouts was picked for the competition, with eight other girls, at the end of that same year. Then came a convocation, with the whole school present and each candidate leading the cheering in turn. After that they voted for the four winners, two boys and two girls. Mary Joe led the list in a walk.

Her summer, Tom remembered, had been devoted to yell rehearsals, meetings to choose costumes, and practice sessions until her first official appearance before the school at the opening football game in late September. Always she and Tom had been close. Now she was against him; she was on the other side. She was helping to keep him off the team and out of the State.

Against his will he was drawn up back of the scoreboard that afternoon to watch the rally—really, of course, to watch Mary Jo. It hurt to see her leading the cheers for those kids and not for him, yet somehow he couldn't stay away. When he reached his perch, the girls were filing in helter-skelter, a dozen at a time pushing into the rows, all dressed in their red-and-white costumes. Evidently they were taking it seriously.

The Midgets hadn't appeared yet; probably Hooks was giving them a blackboard talk. Consequently, they were late reaching the floor. As they raced out, bouncing balls before them, they were greeted by a spontaneous roar. You might have thought the school was welcoming the victors of the State.

Tom saw the boys look up with astonished faces, saw them watch as Mary Jo and the other yell leader raced onto the boards. Slowly he began to understand. This was the school's reply to the petition, the only way they could express their feeling. The idea didn't make him happy, either, for although only a portion of the student body was present, enough of them were on hand to show lots of support behind the new team.

Then, just as the girls of Block R were sitting down, they rose again, shrieking, yelling, and waving their hands. Hooks, in sweat shirt and slacks, the whistle suspended from his neck, was coming out on the floor.

"One-two-three-four . . . who-ya-gonna-yell-for? Barnum . . . Barnum . . . Barnum . . . one-two-three-four . . . Barnum!"

The squad was all over the floor now, shooting at baskets on both sides and both ends of the court, doing a few figure eights up and down the floor. They seemed alive and keener than ever before. The noise from the stands rose, fell, rose, yet never died away. Moreover, more kids kept joining the crowd, filling the seats around Block R, making a large cheering section. Their enthusiasm amazed Tom. He realized that the whole school was not behind the old varsity. He didn't like that thought at all.

Hooks stepped out to say something to one player, and the crowd rose cheering. He paid no attention, but Tom noticed that immediately he moved away and turned his back on them, not wanting anyone to see the tears gathering in his eyes. It was plain to see that he was affected by the demonstration.

Then Mary Jo raced to the center of the floor, Grace Shafer, the other girl yell leader, at her side. Both wore their white sweaters with the big red R in front, their white skirts and shoes. The costume was becoming; it set off the blond hair falling around Mary Jo's shoulders. He had to admit she was easily the prettiest girl in school and the best-liked as well. It was plain she could manage the crowd in the stands; she could bring out the noise as no one else could. As she stood there on tiptoes, her arms went up in front of her face. Immediately three hundred and fifty pairs of hands smacked together; three hundred and fifty voices shouted, "Let's *go*, big team, let's *go*." Clap-clap, clap-clap. "Let's *go*, big team, let's *go*." Clap-clap. "Let's *go*." Clap-clap.

Hooks' whistle pierced the din. Two teams took the floor, the subs in white shirts, the varsity in red. Hang it all, thought Tom, this is unfair. Those are our shirts; that's where we should be. I wonder whether we were right, though, when we told him . . . when we said we wouldn't play. . . .

He watched closely as Coondog and Shorty went in as forwards, Strings at center, and Andy and Randy as guards. He also watched the stands rise, yelling.

"Get hot, team . . . get hot . . . get hot, big team . . . get hot!" they implored.

They kept it up, and to Tom's surprise a change slowly came over the boys on the floor. Gradually, little by little, they caught fire in that electric atmosphere. He could actually feel them become a team, not five separate players but a unit. Their passes were sharp and sure, their screening was sound, their shots hit. Over to Andy, back to Randy. Gosh, that boy is fast! Say, there's a pass for you—over to Coondog, in to Strings, who pivoted suddenly, reached up and popped the ball in.

"Yea, Ridgewood, yea, Ridgewood . . . Let's go, team, let's go!"

Now it seemed as if the whole school was there. The seats on one side were almost filled. It disturbed Tom, made him realize that the kids who had supported him were definitely in the minority. Because a great mass of boys and girls were on hand yelling, and the louder they yelled the better the players responded. It was not merely that they swamped the subs. What Hooks had been unable to do, the gang in the stands were doing. They were making those five individuals into a team right before Tom's astonished eyes.

Hooks ran up and down the floor with them, watching carefully, calling fouls, blowing the whistle and pointing out their mistakes, seeing them come to life as they had never done since they stopped being the B team and became the varsity. This, reflected Tom, is how they played when they were the B team. This is the way they looked the night they beat the Wildcats, confident, sure of themselves, cool, resourceful. He was shaken by what he saw. Play like that, he thought, and they'll go places between now and the end of March.

Only they won't. They'll blow; they'll **crack**

under pressure; they'll quit when they play a game. I know. I've been there before.

By this time he had seen enough to make him feel completely miserable, and so he decided to get out ahead of the crowd. Carefully he climbed down and went back of the stands and out toward the front entrance, wondering whether by any chance Mary Jo could be right. But we weren't soreheads; we didn't act like soreheads. We only wanted Hooks to give us a chance to play against Marbletown. Surely we had earned that. Then what did he do? Chucked us off the squad—that's what he did. Threw us out without a word.

People simply didn't know the facts; they didn't really understand the situation. Yet somehow Tom was less sure now that the petition would really bring about Hooks' resignation. If those kids ever caught fire, if they ever got rolling in a game, things could happen.

Moving toward the front entrance, he was passed by Mr. Schroeder, the superintendent of schools, who walked quickly to the gymnasium door. Leaning against it was Charlie Robbins, the assistant basketball coach, with a stop watch in his hand.

"Hello, Charlie, what goes on? What's all this?"

The roars from the stands, louder than ever, drowned his voice. Over the heads of the two men Tom could see his girl—or the girl who had once been his girl—turn a graceful handspring and come up in time with the other yell leader.

Five hundred voices shouted together, "Let's go, big team, let's *go!*"

"Hey there, Charlie, what's up? What's the idea?" Mr. Schroeder repeated his question to the assistant coach, who hadn't heard him the first time.

Charlie turned, and Tom just caught his answer between yells. "Oh, hello, Mr. Schroeder. Nothing much—merely a few of the kids who didn't choose to sign the petition."

Chapter 12

The school board received the petition from a group appointed by the Quarterbacks Club to present it. They were impressed—so much so that they were paralyzed. Their only action was to schedule a special meeting the next week to consider possible action. For the thing was dynamite; they were afraid to do anything and afraid not to do something. So they ended by appointing a committee of three to meet with the city council to study the whole question. This stall consumed over two weeks' valuable time.

Tom was by no means the only impatient person in town. The downtown experts were after Barnum in force, demanding action, clamoring for a new coach as the team stumbled along into early February. Strangers stopped Little Tom on the street, sympathizing with his position, complaining about Barnum's attitude. Sometimes their questions were irritating.

"That big Elmer Johnson, that colored boy he's got in there at center—he's no Red Blake, Tom."

"You said it. He sure isn't."

"Kinda lazy, isn't he?"

"Oh, I dunno 'bout that." After all, when a guy tries to play basketball on a sandwich and a bottle of milk, when he doesn't get enough to eat, what can you expect?

"Seems to me he acts lazy out on that floor. Whad' he do against Marbletown? Couple of foul throws—wasn't that about all?"

"Sure. He was covered by the best defensive man in the state." Tom came back at him quickly. "That guy really had to hustle all evening to handle him, too." He astonished himself by the feeling behind those words. What did these men downtown know about basketball? They saw the game from a seat in the stands. How could they imagine what it was like to have a giant opponent, arms outstretched, dogging every step you took until the final gun?

"Oh . . . yeah . . . sure . . . I didn't happen to catch the Marbletown game."

Pressure continued to mount daily. The editorials on the front page of the *Sentinel*, which surely expressed the general feeling, became increasingly blunt. "Barnum Should Resign," one was headed. The Quarterbacks Club (composed mainly of men who had plunged in the pool at the start of the season) held special meetings to bring pressure to bear on the school board and council and to work every angle. Still Hooks Barnum worked with the new varsity, showing no signs of leaving. Time was moving fast, too.

Then one evening in early February, when the McWilliams family were together in the living room, the telephone rang, as it had been ringing day and night for weeks. Formerly Little Tom had been the first to jump, for occasionally it used to be Mary Jo calling him. However, she never called any more, and all the telephone calls nowadays came from irate citizens who wanted the mayor to act. Usually he refused to answer them.

However, Big Tom was standing beside the phone that evening and picked it up. His end of the conversation, which lasted a long while, was brief and full of short, exclamatory remarks.

"No! Go on . . . he did? They did?"

"No! He did? You don't say . . . you don't mean it! For Pete's sake! What did he say to that?"

At last he returned to his chair, shaking his head. "Well, it seems the boys in the Quarterbacks Club laid it on the line for your friend Barnum this afternoon."

Little Tom looked up. So somebody was doing something. About time, too. "They did? Gee, Dad, what happened?"

"Well, it appears Bill Engelman and his gang had Barnum down to lunch and told him that Kennedy's brother, who is on the school board at Hammond—you know, they lost their coach last month—wanted him right away, at the same salary."

"Say! That's great, Dad, that's fine! When does he leave? He'll take it, won't he? He knows he isn't wanted any more here in Ridgewood; they must have made that plain. Who'll we get? I wish we'd get that coach from Switz City. I like that man; he knows his basketball. Seems they have only 350 folks in that town, and last year they built him a gym that seats 4000 people. That's what they think of him."

Big Tom paid no attention. He went right on with his story. "Well, they offered him a check for a thousand dollars to clear out, a kind of gift, a sort of farewell present, y'know. Guess it would be worth that and more to some of those men who are in on the pool. But Barnum wasn't buying any of that. He's not the man to take a bribe. They didn't get to first base with him."

Tom's heart sank. How stubborn can a guy get? So Barnum was refusing to leave. He was staying on; consequently, his own chances of getting to play were vanishing. Something ought to be done. Someone ought to go to town on the man and really get him out.

"I'll bet Engelman and those guys won't take that sitting down. They'll get him, one way or another."

His father started to reply but the telephone rang again. Throwing down the paper, he got up to answer it. Little Tom was disconsolate. No doubt about it—that Barnum was tough. He simply didn't know when he wasn't wanted. He couldn't get it through his thick head that folks wanted him to leave. The whole town was yelling for a new coach —except some of those crazy kids in school. Tom was full of his troubles and the consequences of Hooks' refusal to take the Hammond job. Then two words in his father's booming tones brought him up quickly.

"Why, Mary Jo, how are you, dear? Mighty glad to hear from you. We haven't been seeing much of you round here lately. Where you been keeping yourself?"

Trust him to make a crack like that! It was exactly the wrong thing, of course. Tom sat looking at his mother, listening in agony, speculating on how such a blunderer could ever have become mayor of a town like Ridgewood. With a forced heartiness which grated on his son, Big Tom continued. Isn't it awful, Tom thought, when your old man gets clubby with your girl!

Undoubtedly it would have gone on all night had he not snatched the telephone from his father's hands.

Her voice was unusually low and serious. "Tom! I need to see you, right away."

His heart came up in his mouth. She needed him; she wanted to see him. Of course. She'd changed her mind now that she realized the B team had no chance. Perhaps Hooks had seen his mistake at last. He must know what a blunder he made, getting tough with his varsity. Hooks wants the varsity back again. So he's sent Mary Jo to ask us, through me. Well, I'm not going to be easy to get, no sir.

"Look, Tom, I'm at Walgreen's downtown. I'll walk up North Main, down Indiana Avenue to Michigan. You come down Michigan and meet me, will you?"

"O.K."

"Right away. Right now."

"Uh-huh." No sir, he wasn't going to be easy to get. He hung up and went over to the clothes closet in the hall.

"Tom!" His mother called to him. "Be sure and put on overshoes. I think it's started to snow."

This was her usual remark whenever he went out. Wear a jacket; take along a coat; put on your overshoes; don't forget your rubbers.

But just for once his mother was right. It was colder outdoors and snowing hard. Already there were several inches on the sidewalks; the few cars that clanked past all had chains on. He could tell by the fierceness of it that a storm was setting in. For once he felt glad not to be with the team, because returning that night from Lafayette would take hours and hours.

He bundled the collar of his jacket around his neck and plunged into the driving snow, turning at the corner of Walnut and again at the next intersection along Michigan Avenue. His ears tingled in the frosty air, his gloved hands in his pockets were stiff, his toes were icy; but he was warm, happy, and excited inside. He was going to see her again. But she needn't think he was going to be easy to get. He was not!

Then suddenly, right under a street lamp on Michigan, they were together, face to face.

Except in school, where he tried hard not to look at her, this was the first time they had been near each other for over a month. In that time he had almost forgotten how really pretty she was. The snow fringed the red kerchief around her yellow hair, fell over the blue coat which was buttoned around the neck. Never had she seemed so near to him and so attractive. Now things would be all right again, for now she must have realized her mistake.

She was excited, he noticed, as he took her arm and they moved slowly down the street. He felt close to her. The streets were empty—no traffic, no passers-by; they seemed alone in a white, silent world.

"Oh, Tom, the most terrible thing has happened." He turned, amazed, wondering what was up. She went on. "Some goon has smeared great daubs of yellow paint all over Hooks' house. He's at Lafayette tonight, and the place was empty. Who d'you think could have done such a mean, disgusting thing?"

Why, lots of people, he thought. Lots of people in town dislike Hooks Barnum. Yet he hated the idea as much as she did; it was cruel and cowardly, and unfair when he was out of town, besides.

Suddenly she surprised him by changing the subject. "Tom, will you do something for me?"

Here it comes! She wants me back on the team. Will I do something for her? Yes, I'll do anything at all for you. I'll climb Mount Everest, swim the English Channel. I'll get back in there for the Redskins and slip the winning bucket in at the finals of the State. And you'll be there leading the yelling in support of me, just like you did last March.

That's what he was feeling and what he wanted to say. All he could do was squeeze her arm and stammer: "Uh-huh. Sure I will. Whatcha want?"

"Oh, I want this so much, Tom. Please do this for me. That team of Hooks, they've caught hold...."

Fear came over him; his happiness melted away as she was speaking. He became aware that his hands and feet were awfully cold, that his ears tingled more than ever.

"Won't you do this for me, Tom?" She drew closer to him, looking up through the snow, and for a quick moment he felt he would do anything at all she wanted.

Then his uncertainty was uppermost, and he asked, "Do what? What is it, Mary Jo? What do you want me to do?"

"Help with the team, Tom. If you can't play, at least you can help. After this, after they've ruined his house, we owe it to him—the school owes it to him, I mean. Get Joe and Harry and Ned and come out every afternoon and practice with them. You could work with Strings Johnson. You could make him all-state. You could, you know."

So Hooks had not asked her to get them back! The letdown was horrible. Depression surged over him; disappointment smothered him. So she merely wanted him to help with that lousy B team. She just wanted to use him.

"Why should I? What's that team to me?"

Her arm pulled away. "Well, it's the Redskins, after all. You don't want to see them beaten in the first round of the sectionals next week, do you? At least they must come through the sectionals. Please help, Tom, you can help so much. . . ."

"I don't care whether they come through the sectionals or not, whether they win or lose. They'll get trimmed tonight by the Broncos. They'll get badly beaten next week in the sectionals by Central City; that is, if they ever get past the first round. Which I doubt. Those kids aren't the Redskins— You know that. *We're* the Redskins, Harry and Ned and Joe and me."

She looked at him through the snow. Her tone was as cold as the air he breathed. "Still sore, aren't you, Tom? Still sore."

"So all right," he replied, anger in his voice. "I'm sore. What's it to me if some clown painted up Barnum's house? He had it coming to him."

"Oh, Tom!" She was shocked. He had really shocked her now. "Just a bunch of soreheads, that's what you boys are. Cutting up people's car tires, smearing paint on houses—that's your idea of fun, I s'pose."

She was angry, but he was furious. Because he saw she believed he had done those things, or at least had a hand in them. She should have known better. Mary Jo Berry, the girl who had been Little Tom's girl since they came together to junior high. At that moment he could feel her clinging to him, her feet in the air, on the gym steps the night of the celebration after the State.

"All right, Mary Jo, if that's the way you feel, if that's how you feel about things, good night."

He turned abruptly, walked rapidly away through the thickening snow, and turned the corner of Michigan toward home. His feet hurt, so did his hands and ears. Other things inside hurt more.

Chapter 13

The petition! Why doesn't the school board act? Why don't they do something about the petition, asked everyone in town. Hardly two days went by now without a front-page spread in the *Sentinel* calling on the school board to "Give Ridgewood the Kind of Team It Deserves." Meaning, of course, fire Barnum and let another coach put back the victorious veterans of the previous year. But this issue was dynamite in town. The school board met, talked, argued, and got nowhere.

All the while Slim Harris, the sports editor of the *Sentinel*, adopted a tone of condescension toward the team in his daily column. He seldom wasted space explaining that the process of making a basketball player takes time and effort by all concerned, that it was going on steadily every afternoon in the field house. Instead, he gave the impression that the Redskins were still an inept bunch, falling over their feet and shooting wildly from the floor, as they had done earlier in the season.

With almost 800 basketball teams in the tournament, no human being could possibly see them all between the end of November and the first of March. Consequently, the sports editors of other newspapers throughout the state read Slim Harris each day in the *Sentinel* and followed his line about the Ridgewood varsity.

Yes, they all agreed, too bad the Redskins won't be in there this season. Now it looks like Evansville Bosse, South Bend Central, Marbletown, or Fort Wayne. Of course Sid Clements has a good bunch of boys at Anderson, and so has the new man at Lafayette.

On the night when the Redskins were playing at Anderson, one of the last regular games of the season before the tournament began, things came to a head in town. The showdown could no longer be delayed.

The school board, split down the middle over the petition, unable to decide whether to fire Hooks and get a new coach or not, had referred the whole problem to the city council. That meant the issue was so important that they were afraid to act, therefore they had passed the buck. Everyone understood, but lots of folks in town were angry, for they wanted action.

The problem demanded attention, and the next council meeting was three weeks away. So the mayor had decided to call an open meeting and discuss the whole situation at the city hall. The only available evening was the night of the game over at Anderson. By midafternoon it had become apparent that the small room in the city hall would not be large enough to hold the gang who wanted Barnum's scalp. So the meeting was transferred to the high-school auditorium.

Jackson Grant, the janitor, stood near the doorway and shook his head as the crowd pushed past him. "I never saw anything like this, I surely never did. They come out to the Marbletown game this way, but never to a meeting before."

At eight-thirty that evening, with the auditorium packed, people jammed in the rear, and an angry crowd surging outside of the closed doors, it became necessary to move over to the field house, which fortunately was empty that night.

The first thing Tom saw as he came in was a huge sign hanging down in front, *Barnum Resign*. Hanging from the rear balcony was another large sign, *Put Ridgewood Back in the State*.

Seated with the Quarterbacks Club in the middle of the floor, Tom saw the crowd meant business. They had not come just for fun; they were there for blood, to get action, to get that man Barnum out.

After all, he came from Marbletown originally; maybe he wasn't a Communist himself, but there were a lot of them over there. That's how the men around Tom were talking.

Sometimes the town merchants stayed away from open meetings and ducked controversial issues—but not tonight. Tom saw lots of them nearby. There was a kind of ugly feeling in the air, a feeling he couldn't exactly explain and didn't exactly like.

When the mayor, with Mr. Hitchcock, the principal, and Mr. Schroeder, the superintendent of schools, came through the door in the rear of the arena and onto the platform, a sullen roar swept the place. Tom noticed immediately that his father looked angry and upset. The thing was getting under his skin. He stood fumbling with some papers while the other two men seated themselves behind a table. On it were a mike, a gavel, a pitcher of water, and some glasses. Then he stepped up and took hold of the microphone.

There was no affection in the crowd's greeting as there had been at gatherings during the previous year, and they did not listen respectfully as they had done before. Instead, shouts and cries rose over the hall and swept away the sound of his voice.

Several thousand voices chanted in unison, "We want action! We want action!" Their feet banged the floor; their voices echoed over the big hall.

Big Tom stood waiting awhile, flushed and resentful. As the disorder continued and showed no signs of stopping, he seized the gavel and pounded upon the table. Little Tom, on the floor, could see the table shake, yet heard no sound but the noise from those around him.

"The meeting will please come to order!" The mayor glared angrily, with no result. "The meeting will come to order," he shouted into the mike.

But the meeting had other ideas; the meeting refused to come to order, and although after a while the noise lessened somewhat, there was still a hum and buzz of conversation over the entire hall. Once again the mayor banged furiously. Once again the table shook under his blows.

"We called this meeting . . . this meeting was called . . . to discuss the problem of our basketball coach . . ."

"Barnum . . . resign!"

"Throw him out!"

"Make Barnum resign!"

A burst of derision greeted Big Tom. The mob's tone, their whole attitude meant utter defiance. He shook his mane of black hair, and Tom knew that now his father was thoroughly aroused. "You bunch of hoodlums!" he roared above the din.

The noise subsided, diminished, suddenly died away. It was as if he had smacked them full in the face and they had fallen back, speechless and stunned. They were stunned both by his words and by the anger on his usually jovial face.

"I mean that, too. You people lost your senses? Have you? What's the matter with you? What's come over this town? There's been enough vandalism and rowdy stuff among the kids lately, and there isn't going to be any more, either. We'll hold this meeting in an orderly way—or not at all."

Just a few faint handclaps—not many or loud—were the answer. Most of the crowd, however, settled into a kind of half silence as he stood there glaring at them from the platform. Because everyone knew Big Tom meant what he said, that he was quite capable of adjourning the meeting for two weeks and walking out of the hall. Since the crowd wanted action above everything, they listened in that half quiet, a sort of low murmur going through the place.

Let's hurry up and get Barnum out. The heck with all this talking, they seemed to be saying.

"Everyone present knows what I'm referring to." The mayor's icy tones could be clearly heard now. "The home of our basketball coach has been striped with yellow paint, his car tires have been slashed, and this evening . . . I've just heard . . . this evening, while he's over at Anderson with the team, all the windows of his house have been broken with BB shot."

There was a change in the feverish atmosphere; the arena became less explosive. The tension was just as tight as ever, but quiet came now. Everyone in the gymnasium listened.

"We haven't any idea who did it. However, the police have instructions from me to find out. I intend to track this thing down if it's the last thing I ever do."

Folks stirred uneasily in their seats. Had this been done by school kids, was it some of the heavy betters in the pool, or had outsiders done it? Maybe folks from Marbletown. Why not? Surely a kid wouldn't dare shoot a gun into a man's living room!

The crowd listened now as the mayor continued. "In the meantime, Jack Curtis has stationed a patrolman at Barnum's house and we'll keep one there until the end of the season."

Little Tom knew how his father hated this sort of thing; it upset and angered him. He noticed the rustle of the papers as they shook in his hand. But he had control of the mob now; his anger had subdued and quieted everyone on the floor and in the balconies.

"As you are all aware, the team is playing over at Anderson this evening, and Hooks Barnum could not be with us. Unfortunately, this was the only evening we could meet for the next ten days. So he left me a letter to read.

"'Dear Mr. Mayor. This is to inform you that I resign as coach of the Ridgewood High School basketball team . . .'"

The roar was overpowering, piercing—like that frenzied cry when the team slips in a bucket in the last seconds of a close game. The noise rose over the arena, sudden, triumphant in tone.

There! There, they all seemed to be saying. Barnum's quitting. He's quitting at last. Now get those boys back in there tomorrow; get Little Tom and the other veterans back again. If we're gonna win the State next month, they better go down and climb into their suits right now.

The mayor stood looking at them. There was a kind of amused smile on his lips as he waited, glancing over the disorderly hall, where everybody was talking to his neighbor and congratulating him. As the noise persisted, he cracked his gavel on the table, again . . . and again . . . and again.

"I hadn't finished reading this letter."

Instantly a groan rose. Some of them understood immediately. There was a catch in it.

"'This is to inform you that I resign as coach of the Ridgewood High School basketball team . . . on the day after the finals. Hooks Barnum, Coach.'"

Boos, catcalls, hisses, jeers. A blurred sound that became words; words that became a sentence; a sentence that became a demand, an ultimatum.

"Barnum resign . . . Barnum resign . . . Barnum resign . . ." Several thousand people took up the chant, pounding the backs of the balcony seats, stamping on the floor. The sound swept the arena, echoed back from the rafters in the roof. "Barnum resign . . . Barnum resign . . ."

Up on the platform the mayor waited patiently until they tired slightly and the din lessened. Then he smacked the table hard with his gavel. At first Tom could hear nothing; then the sound of his father's pounding came through the roar. There he stood, flushed, annoyed, whacking and whacking until the shouting lessened and his voice could be heard.

"There'll be none of this pressure stuff tonight. I've had all the pressure on me these past weeks I'm going to take. We're all interested in our team in this town; that's fine. But we'll hold this meeting in an orderly manner. I've agreed to let each side of the question have three minutes to present their views; then we'll open the meeting for discussion. The group who want a new basketball coach have chosen as their speaker . . ." He paused, looking at them.

"Tom McWilliams."

Chapter 14

This was a smart move. Instead of some prominent citizen, some downtown better or a member of the Quarterbacks Club, they had chosen one of the most popular boys on the team to present their case, a boy known to everyone in town. Moreover, he was the mayor's son.

From below he pushed and shoved, rather red of face, and worked his way through the crowd to the steps at the side of the platform, drawing a terrific amount of applause as he came up. Everyone wanted to show how they sympathized with him. Yet although Little Tom had been coached and drilled and was full of a sense of injustice, it was not easy, he discovered, to be up there before 6000 people for the first time.

No longer was he a cool, competent giant out on the floor in white shorts with a big number six on his red shirt; he was an embarrassed, awkward boy in a plaid shirt open at the neck and an old pair of pants.

Clutching the mike with both hands as if it were a post, he stammered, "Well, folks, we . . . now . . . this is how we fellas feel. We all feel it's mighty unfair to chuck a boy out of school for doing what just about everybody in town does every day of the baseball season."

This was greeted by a burst of cheers and yells. There wasn't anyone in the crowd who didn't know he was talking about the daily pools and the betting that went on at Mac and Joe's Grill and the other spots along Indiana Avenue. However, this support did not seem to relax Tom—quite the contrary. He fumbled with his pockets, ran his hand through his thick hair, stood on one foot, and wound one leg around the other until he was tied up in a knot.

"We think Red Blake got a mighty raw deal, and we said so, that's all!" With great tact he omitted any reference to the varsity's having broken training. "We got up . . . that is . . . I mean to say, the town presented a petition with over 10,000 signatures to the school board for action. And lots and lots of us kids at school worked on it, too. But the board, they just did nothing. We feel this is unfair . . . we feel the coach . . . has become a dictator."

The inference was that winning the State had gone to Hooks Barnum's head. This last remark brought a volume of applause, a burst of noise, of feet stamping and cheers. A dictator! Of course,

a kind of Hitler, a man who threw boys off the
varsity for no reason at all, a man who was un-Amer-
ican. To the members of the Quarterbacks Club
bunched together in the center of the floor, the
logic was obvious. They listened, giving him far
more respect and attention than they had given his
father, notwithstanding the boy's lack of assurance
and his obvious stage fright.

Then, anxious to end the agony and get back to
the anonymity of the crowd on the floor, Tom
continued hastily, pouring the words out, speaking
much too fast. "And so . . . we fellas . . . we feel
the mayor of this town has a duty . . . we think
he ought to take action tonight to ask for the
coach's resignation . . . and get a new man . . .
a good man . . . and do what the people of Ridgewood want."

Obviously the people of Ridgewood there in the
field house that evening did want this, too. Anybody
could see as much. They cheered with warmth and
emotion as Little Tom stumbled down with evident
relief from the platform, mopping his face with a
handkerchief as he went along the rows of seats
to his place in the middle of the Quarterbacks Club
on the floor.

Voices called over approvingly, men slapped him
on the back and clapped his shoulders, proud to

know the team's basketball hero, who was able to challenge his own dad, the mayor.

"Attaboy, Little Tom, you said something."

"Nice work, Tom."

"Great going there, Little Tom. You sure told your old man where he gets off."

Up on the platform the mayor rose again. He went into no act, made no introduction; he simply said, "Mary Jo Berry, who presents the other side."

Most folks who attended basketball games in Ridgewood—and that meant about everyone in town who could walk—knew Mary Jo Berry.

"You remember her, don't you? She's the chief yell leader, that pretty blonde who wears the white skirt and the white sweater with the big red R, the one with the nice legs who does handsprings out before the cheering section?"

"Yes, of course; I know. Isn't she Tom McWilliams' girl? Oh . . . she isn't any more? They've bust up? Oh, I see."

Even her entrance was different. While Little Tom had come stumbling over people's feet and legs as he worked his way up to the platform, she walked calmly out from the back, where the mayor had entered, and came to the microphone cool and completely at ease.

Mary Jo was only a girl, yet that evening she was a girl no longer. Something had happened; she was

different; she had grown up. The crowd expected
to see her in white skirt and white sweater, but that
night she was a young lady in a dark-blue suit
which set off her figure extremely well, sober, trim,
good-looking. Her hair no longer hung over her
shoulders. It was arranged in such a way that every
woman present—and there were lots of them—knew
she had spent the afternoon in Doris's Beauty Salon
on West Michigan. Moreover, she was a contrast
to Little Tom because she was used to facing crowds;
crowds meant nothing at all to her, and that noisy
throng in the field house bothered her not in the
least.

The mob quieted down as she stood silently
looking at them, picking out the kids in the balcony
and glancing at the kids scattered over the floor,
self-possessed and poised. The crowd might yell at
the mayor or the superintendent of schools but
before this pretty young woman they were quiet
and respectful. You could hear every word she
uttered.

"Friends, I'm speaking for the kids of Ridgewood
High." She stopped and looked them over again, up
and down, in the balcony and on the floor, her eyes
sweeping the crowd, as if to say, "Anyone like to
take me up on that? Anybody think different? Anyone got anything to say?"

Nobody had, so in deep silence she went on. "We kids in school all know Hooks Barnum. Some of us have known him for a long time and seen him work, not only with the basketball team but with us all, with everybody. We love him; we want him to stay as our coach. Not just because we love him; but because we think . . ."

Hang it, she's a sweet girl, isn't she? What on earth's the matter with Little Tom? What's biting him?

She hesitated, handling the mike like an old trouper, looking across the silent hall, her chin raised. You could see something was coming; you could see she was going to deliver a punch line. It came.

"But because we think he did the right thing last fall . . . when he threw . . . a bunch of soreheads . . . off the varsity."

A murmur ran over the arena. Wow! Say, that's talking! That's sure laying it on the line! Folks glanced at each other quickly. Everyone sat up; the tension grew; the big field house became electric. Why, she's calling Little Tom a sorehead! Say, what d'you think of that? She was his girl, wasn't she? Wonder how he'll take that.

Then came a stir below. A chair scraped and a big, gangling figure rose to his feet, his face flushed. Little Tom was so angry that for a moment he could find no words. At last he spoke, his tone dry and hard, his voice cracking with emotion.

"I'd just like to ask the speaker one thing. She claims to speak for the kids in school. Well, she doesn't speak for me or for any of us fellas that were thrown off the varsity unfairly last November. I'd like to ask her to prove she speaks for the kids in school."

He subsided quickly. Heads turned back from him to the girl on the platform. Guess he has her there, all right! Oh, he's smart, Little Tom is; he's got the old man in him. He was always a quick thinker on the court. Remember that last quarter of the Marbletown game a year ago?

She glared down, speechless. Yes, he had her there. For after all, how *could* you prove such a thing, how could you be sure? She should never have made that crack about speaking for the kids in school. Too bad. She's a nice girl, only she didn't think fast enough.

Then her voice came clear and lovely across the arena. "Yes, I will. I'll prove to everyone in this room now that I'm speaking for the kids in school, all except a few, a few who didn't get their own way, so they go round town making trouble and calling the coach a dictator." She looked down at him—hard.

Boy, she's tough, that girl. Nobody could misunderstand how she felt.

"Jerry! Norman! Bring them up here."

All heads turned. Two big boys, each carrying a carton in his arms, worked through the crowd to the steps at the side. Necks stretched; faces peered. Slowly the two came up toward the center of the stage and banged the boxes down on the table.

Now what? What on earth is in them?

"I've been asked to prove that I speak for the kids of Ridgewood High. Here is the proof. In the last six days, we've collected in school . . . sixty-five dollars . . . and fifty-two cents, mostly in dimes and nickels, nothing larger than a quarter, from just about everyone in the school. We're buying new tires for Hooks Barnum's car."

She turned, plunging her hands into each box. Coins fell through her fingers: quarters, dimes, nickels, and pennies, hundreds of them, clinking and clanking and tinkling as they fell back into each box. As they fell, a quick burst of spontaneous applause rang out over the packed hall.

Folks in Ridgewood like fair play. Nobody in town was exactly happy about those slashed tires.

Then something happened. A boy, waving a paper in his outstretched hand, was trying to get her attention from the floor, moving through the crowd toward the platform, shoving and pushing.

Now she saw him and stood waiting, poised, perfectly at ease as the applause died away.

Yes, it's fine of the kids to chip in and buy new tires for Barnum; that's great. But somehow it really doesn't settle the problem of the new coach.

Finally the boy reached the front where folks were seated almost up to the platform. The three men behind the table peered down with interest; so did the vast crowd above and below. The clock on the scoreboard showed 9:32 as she took the paper from his hand, glanced at it, straightened up.

"Final score tonight over in Anderson." Her face was expressionless.

Come on, come on, did we win? Did we lose? Of course we lost, sure we lost. We couldn't beat the Anderson Indians with that B team. Why, they've been picked to go all the way to the State.

"Final score in Anderson tonight." No one stirred, nobody moved, not a chair creaked on the floor. The silence was far more intense, much more meaningful than the volume of noise earlier that evening.

"Anderson, 44." A groan rose that cut her short. Usually the winning score was given first, so everyone there knew the team had been trounced. What did you expect with the B team, with the Davis twins and that big colored boy, that Strings Johnson? Barnum is nuts, chucking away a winning team like that.

"Anderson, 44. Ridgewood . . . 49."

The place exploded. You couldn't hear, you couldn't think. The hall became a vast, heaving sea of emotion, of waving hands and arms. Here and there, downstairs and up in the balcony, kids began chanting, "We want Barnum . . . we want Barnum . . . we want Barnum!"

She didn't move or attempt to direct them; she just stood there, a radiant figure with a happy smile. Yet somehow the words seemed to come through at her direction.

"We want Barnum . . . we want Barnum!"

It was louder because they were not together in a cheering section, so the noise came from all over the place. Nobody could possibly doubt that Mary Jo Berry spoke for the kids of Ridgewood High.

The mayor rose. No use going on now. Because the meeting was breaking up by itself; people in the rear were leaving. The crowd was dissolving, slowly at first, then faster; they were turning back toward the doors and the front entrance. Yes, the meeting was adjourning itself.

Well, well. Whadda ya know! Whadda ya think of that? Barnum's Midgets trimmed Anderson. Say, those Davis twins can't be so bad after all!

Chapter 15

Sentiment after the Anderson game was still coolish toward Hooks Barnum, but interest in the petition seemed to be less intense, and the general feeling around town was that the coach should be left alone until after the sectionals next week.

He himself realized he had two problems. First, he had to give a bunch of kids from the B team confidence. That was easy to say, hard to accomplish. Because a team only acquires confidence by battling through to victory in an important contest. Yet you cannot win a big match without that inner faith. Until the Anderson game the week before the sectionals, the Redskins had not trimmed a single first-class team.

The second problem was more difficult. Hooks' system had always stressed possession basketball. With a short and speedy squad it was necessary to change to a fast-breaking game, for only by mastering the fast break could these boys hope to make any showing in the sectionals.

The tournament began on the Thursday after Washington's Birthday. In the state of Indiana, all the games before the tournament are practice games, make-believe, trial runs. Once tournament play starts, everything is different. It's dog eat dog and no holds barred and the devil take the loser. Business stops in town while the businessmen speculate about the team. The local newspaper puts basketball on the front page and other news on page two. School-work becomes a routine affair.

The tournament started, then, with the sixty-four sectionals held in various centers throughout the whole state. At Ridgewood, on the first after-noon, the smaller townships like Milton and Econ-omy and Webster fought it out for the doubtful pleasure of facing the larger and tougher teams. Yet although these smaller teams might not even win their first match and had no chance whatever of coming through, they all wanted to play against the big boys.

Little Tom determined not to show at the field house that week end. It hurt to watch the team on the floor without him and another player wearing his number six, so the first two days he merely listened to the scores at night over the air. On Friday afternoon the Redskins defeated Fountain City. In the evening Central City won its match easily. Ridgewood got past Williamsburg in a close game on Saturday afternoon, while Central City disposed of Greensfork.

When Red Blake came to the house that evening and suggested they might as well run over and watch Central City put the extinguisher on Barnum and the kids, Tom, who wanted to go yet didn't want to go, either, agreed. But he knew they would both enjoy watching the well-drilled visitors pour it onto those unfortunate kids. So the two boys took the mayor's tickets, which were for seats exactly in the center of the stands under Block R; then, since neither wished to be conspicuous, they climbed up to seats under the rafters.

Red looked about, a hunk of popcorn in his hand. There was plenty of space around them. "If we hadda been out on that-there floor tonight, think you'd see all those empty seats? Like fun!"

Little Tom agreed glumly. Several folks around noticed them, nudged their neighbors, and pointed out the two boys. Heads turned curiously in their direction. This made Tom uncomfortable. He felt worse when Mary Jo appeared in her white sweater and skirt. Soon afterward the Redskins took the floor, with Shorty McCall wearing his own familiar number six.

Tom observed from the opening toss that Central City was not in the least fooled by the gags and jokes about Barnum's Midgets. They had scouted

Ridgewood, and they knew that although this was not the victorious varsity of the previous year, any Barnum team would be well coached and hard to take. So they were ready with a squad of good shooters, excellent ball handlers, fast-breaking, tough players.

Tom soon saw something only to be recognized by someone who had been in competitive basketball himself. The kids, the B team—that gang of juniors who had become the varsity overnight—started to take hold. They were a team with poise and resources at last. You had to know each man and feel the change to realize this.

Yet there it was. The game began with each team feeling the other out; and the score went along evenly, Central City hitting first, going ahead two points, being tied, and then taking the lead once more.

"That Strings Johnson is taking an awful beating under that basket," remarked Tom, his eyes on the floor.

"Sure is. I give him another quarter to quit cold. He hasn't got it; never did have it," agreed Red.

The first quarter ended with Central City leading 16-13. By this time Tom had completely revised his estimate of the team. He saw that in Andy and Randy Davis Ridgewood had two of the best dribblers and the fastest scooters in the business. Central City had some fast boys, yet both twins were running around them. No wonder those kids gave us trouble in practice games, Tom thought. They're good. If Barnum could only make a jumping center like Red out of that big colored boy, the team could cause trouble tonight.

By the middle of the second quarter the twins caught fire. They were dribbling all over the floor, slipping in baskets from every angle. Basketball is a game of movement and they were moving—sparking the whole team with their run-and-shoot tactics. The Central City boys were taller and heavier. They were older and more experienced. Yet they were not enjoying themselves.

"Look! Look! See that?" Tom suddenly grabbed Red's arm, admiration in his tone.

It was a dazzling play, a gem of quick thinking and quicker reflexes. In a scramble for the ball, Andy saw Randy was open, stabbed at it as if playing volley ball, and punched it directly into Randy's arms.

Randy fairly ate up the floor, dribbling now with one hand, now with the other, reversing himself, dodging a guard, and going under to hit with a two-handed shot that put Ridgewood ahead for the first time in the game. Tom glanced at Red. Red raised his eyebrows. They were both thinking the same thing.

Mary Jo danced out on the floor, and below the two boys Block R rose as a unit, shrieking. "The Red . . . the White . . . the team . . . let's fight!"

For a second or two Tom had difficulty concentrating on the game as he watched her. When he looked back, Central City was taking the ball out and, as he expected, went ahead almost immediately. Class tells, he thought. Yet he felt sure the outcome was still open. You had to admit those kids were playing coolly and well.

The third quarter was brutal. Ridgewood suddenly got hot and caught up at 39 apiece. Central City went ahead on a free throw and it was 40-39 in their favor when the final quarter started in an explosion of noise from the stands. Then a break came. In the first minute the best Central City player, their star forward, fouled out. Shorty sank the free throw and a second later Strings got up on the backboard to snag a rebound, flipped the ball over to Andy who was off down the floor, drove under, and scored with a lay-up to put Ridgewood ahead, 42-40.

"The lucky bum," sneered Red.

"Yeah," said Tom, his eyes on the floor and the shifting pattern of the players under the Ridgewood basket. But in his heart he knew that luck often comes to the team that stays in there trying, and he could see that the twins were running the legs off the bigger team. They were playing much better than in the first half, too.

Now Central City tried a long throw-in, but Strings tipped it over to Randy, who brought it quickly down the floor, the others panting at his heels. A pass to Andy, over to Coondog, back to Randy, who cut into the corner . . . was blocked . . . passed out to Andy, who flipped the ball to Strings in the circle.

The big chap pivoted quickly and threw. It was a well-timed one-hander that plopped through the net and put Ridgewood four points ahead with only three and a half minutes to go.

Down below, Mary Jo, her blond hair streaming behind, danced onto the floor, and Block R rose, shouting in unison.

"Let's go . . . Big Team . . . let's go . . .
You can do it, Big Team . . . you know!"

Everyone was pounding the boards with their feet, for the field house saw victory ahead. Unexpected, unbelievable—yet victory was there, in plain view. The rumble-dumble of thousands of pairs of heels and the noise of thousands of voices added to the confusion. Now Central City, hot, tired, mouths open, brought the ball out in desperation. They had anticipated a tough, hard-fought contest; but since

they had beaten last year's Ridgewood varsity early
in the season, they naturally felt sure of beating
the new team and qualifying for the regionals next
week at Marbletown for the first time in Central
City's history.

Yet with only a few minutes left, they were
behind, run off their feet by a couple of kids who
hardly reached their shoulders. Central City was
supposed to be a fast team. The Davis twins could
run faster—and longer. They were a two-man riot
act on the floor, with a sound supporting cast.

Tom watched, wondering to himself who would
crack first. He was so emotionally involved that it
hurt to see that familiar, ever-changing pattern on
the floor below. He had come that night to see the
team that had beaten him and his teammates swamp
these fresh kids. Then, as the twins hung on, as
they raced around their bigger opponents, his admiration for them altered his feelings.

Now he almost wanted them to win. He hoped
they would lose, yet he hoped they would win.
In fact, he began praying through those agonizing
minutes, as the two squads battled fiercely in the
last minutes of play, that Ridgewood might come
through.

Then another foul was called on Central City.
Their coach, angry and upset, leaped from his bench,
protesting. Tom had half expected it; he could see

the visitors were worn down now, fighting stubbornly yet blindly.

Cool as a hunk of ice, big Strings stepped to the line and hit both shots. Then Andy and Randy took the game over. First one would cut, then the other, until Central City never knew who had the ball or where it was coming from. They were everywhere on the court, dribbling, faking, feinting, ducking in under the basket every time Ridgewood got the ball. The score mounted rapidly. There could be no doubt now, for their defense was, as always, excellent. Central City was bottled up and unable to shoot. Yet they had to shoot, because they were behind and the last minutes of the game were ticking away on the big electric clock overhead.

Below Tom and Red, the Ridgewood stands were a weaving, bobbing, shrieking, and shouting mass of confusion. The final seconds came. The gun sounded —sharp, sudden, brutal.

The Redskins would be playing in the regionals at Marbletown next week.

High in the stands the two boys looked down on the delirious scene below. Because it was so entirely unexpected, the joy of the boys and girls was as great as if the team had won the finals of the State.

"Well," said Red, "well, whadda ya know? Those lucky bums! Imagine catching Central City off their game like that! Figure that one. What a break for

Barnum! Last week this town was just waiting until Saturday night to chop his head off. Now he's in the regionals, the lucky stiff. Is that guy lucky!"

"I'll say he's lucky. Those two Central men who fouled out there at the end made the difference. Their subs were no good at all. Gee, I wish we could play those kids. I bet we'd beat 'em today by ten points. They wouldn't run on us that way, they wouldn't."

"Are you crazy? Are you blowing your lid? Are you nuts, Tom? We'd beat 'em by twenty points. I'd sure like to take 'em on. Barnum wouldn't allow it; he'd be scared."

"Yeah," said Tom, watching Block R in ecstasy below, waving and shouting for their tired but triumphant team on the floor, who were going up the ladder now, cutting down the nets, handing out pieces to each player.

"Sectionals . . . regionals . . . semifinals . . . finals. Sectionals . . . regionals . . . semifinals . . . finals. Sectionals . . . regionals . . . semifinals . . . finals!" shouted the girls of Block R, echoing each word with a collective stamp of their feet. "Sectionals . . . regionals . . . semifinals . . . finals!"

Chapter 16

Ridgewood's victory did not go unnoticed throughout the state.

"Say, what about those Ridgewood boys chopping up Central City?"

Barnum's Midgets—that had been quite a gag, a great joke. Now it wasn't so funny.

"Seems like those Redskins are tough. They can really run with that ball; they play that fast break well." This was how people talked now about the team.

Tom happened to be standing outside the Davis drugstore on Indiana Avenue the afternoon following the sectionals. Several kids from school met him and stopped to ask his opinion of the Central City game.

Tom answered without hesitation. "Why, the lucky stiffs! Were those guys lucky! They caught Central City on a bad night. You know how it is; the best teams have bad nights like that. Then if

Chester hadn't fouled out in the last quarter . . . boy, that team of ours was just shot through with luck, all the time, every minute of the game."

"You really mean that, Tom McWilliams?"

He whirled about and looked down, quite a long way down. Andy Davis, coming round the corner at that exact moment, had heard his last sentence. "You mean that? You think we won because we were lucky?"

Andy was upset. Yet Tom didn't spare him. "Lucky! Boy, you guys couldn't hold Central City like that again in a hundred years." It was a spiteful thing to say and he knew it, but the words came out before he could hold himself in.

As he expected, Andy bristled. "Why, you know better'n that, Little Tom. Shoot, I wish we could show you big lugs up. I'd like to take you on in a practice game. You'd be surprised . . . you'd see."

"Suit us just fine. I'll promise to get the gang together any time you say after next Saturday." The implication was plain to the circle of open-mouthed kids who stood listening. Tom meant that he expected the team to be beaten in the regionals and out of the State the next week end.

"We're gonna win over in Marbletown, Tom," said Andy with assurance. "Why don't you fellas come round and give us some practice for Saturday?"

Tom disliked the tone of his voice as well as his brash confidence. "Suits me," he said shortly. "You fix it up with Hooks and we'll be glad to show you how to play basketball any time you're ready."

Andy did not wait long with the idea; in fact, he went to the coach's house that afternoon. At first Hooks laughed at him; then, after thinking it over, he began to see such a game might be useful. The B team had never been a soft touch for the varsity in practice, and if they managed to win it would give them a lift that might send them into the Marbletown game in high. For there would be proof that the Central City victory was no fluke. Such a contest, he knew, would be a test of character as much as a test of basketball. But suppose they lost. Well, to lose to the former state champions was surely no disgrace.

So the next morning in school, Hooks stopped Tom. "That's a fine idea, Tom, that practice game. You know, you boys can really help us a lot." Tom shifted uneasily, for his motive was hardly that of helping the varsity.

Hooks continued in his even tones. "Tell you what. We'll have a regulation game of thirty-two minutes—a timer, a referee, the whole works. We'll play tomorrow at three. It'll do us a lot of good if you care to practice in a real game."

The eagerness with which he accepted the chal-

lenge was not exactly reassuring to Tom. He thought
a minute. "But, Hooks, we haven't been together
as a team or had any team practice for a couple of
months. I don't think it's fair for us to go on
without a good workout. We should have a day's
workout first."

Hooks considered this. "Yes, you have a point,
Tom; that's only fair. Let's see now. We have to
use the gym tomorrow. Tell you what. Get your
boys together and I'll see they have the junior high
school gym all afternoon. How's that?"

Consequently, the former varsity had a strenuous
workout together that next afternoon. The following day they took the floor. Hooks held the watch.
Max Thomas, the junior-high coach, was referee.
The champs, the winners of the State, were in
substitute uniforms, and the former B team were
in the varsity suits.

It was as close to a regular game as possible. Word
got around school and fully half the kids were on
hand that afternoon, making it seem like the real
thing. Nobody could doubt where their sympathies
lay; they all wanted the new varsity to win. Certainly, too, no teams ever wanted to win more than
those ten boys struggling against each other that day
in the Ridgewood field house.

Barnum's teams had been famous all over Indiana
as being deliberate players, for stressing possession

basketball—not for them the fast break and the wild heaves. When you have the ball, Hooks insisted, the other team cannot score. He said it a hundred times each season. Yet from the moment Max Thomas tossed the tip-off exactly at three o'clock, the veterans were up against powerhouse basketball.

They had expected this; they had all watched the team in the sectionals, so it was no surprise. Since they had met plenty of firehouse fives before—met them, cooled them off, and tamed them in the end— they were not in the least worried. In fact, they came onto the court with confidence, secure in themselves and their proven ability. After all, they were still the champs.

But basketball is a game of movement. From the start the varsity ran, and from the start they scored. They raced from one end of the court to the other and, because they did, made opportunities to shoot. Whenever they had a chance at the buckets, they usually hit, too. Speed, the veterans expected—not that accurate shooting from any side and every angle.

Tom soon realized that the twins, especially, had become better shots than he had realized. Andy began with a basket from the corner, another on a stolen pass; and between them the two stuffed in seven points in the first quarter, leading 16-9. Then Andy hit again with a one-hander, Randy swiped another pass and went under to count, and the score mounted. Those two little pepperpots, full of fire, were all over the court, dancing and shouting, "Hey . . . hey!" Meaning, "I'm open to shoot. Pass the ball."

Tom called time and the vets stood panting, their arms on each others' shoulders. "Let 'em run. They'll run themselves into the ground if they keep that up."

"Yeah, let 'em run," said Red. "We'll cool 'em off."

Trouble was, they proved to be hard to stop. The twins could dribble with either hand and, as Tom recalled with some dismay, they could both pivot and change direction like lightning. It was disconcerting to play against such speed. In addition, the kids seemed unable to miss that afternoon. And at first the veterans couldn't hit. When the whistle blew for the half, the score was 28-22 against them.

The youngsters had the old varsity dressing room, while Tom and his team huddled outside in a corner formed by the main lockers. A dozen boys followed them curiously and stood watching as they sat down on the hard benches, mopping their wet faces, panting, tired. It was rough, tough basketball; yet none of them were in the least worried. Why should they be? They had outfought and outguessed too many big teams; they had come from behind too often in really big matches to worry now.

Only Tom saw the danger. "Look, you guys, we aren't hitting out there. Joe! You didn't switch this last quarter twice in a row. You gave Andy two buckets. We aren't moving, either. Shucks, if you stand there and let 'em go past, if you let 'em screen us out like that . . .

"Red, you're playing Strings. O.K., he's got three fouls on him now. What you doing on offense? You're out around the foul line. We can't feed you; we can't hit you with the ball out there. Get closer."

Red wiped his face. "Yeah, I'll get closer. That Strings can jump. Why, I never knew he could go up there like that. What's come over him? He must have rubber in his legs."

Tom continued. "Fellas, we just aren't hitting—any of us—we're all careless. Like that first half in the finals last year, against South Bend, remember? Our passes are bad, too. Hit him with the ball; don't throw it away. Harry, you took two bad shots that last quarter. Ned, you took three. Gosh, we shouldn't lose to these kids."

"Relax, Tom," said Red. "We won't. We'll go to town this half. We'll start hitting."

Hooks stuck his head around the corner. "Three minutes, fellas."

"O.K. Thanks, Hooks. Now we've been playing about forty per cent of our game. Let's all snap into it. Let's quit this sloppy playing; let's make every pass good; let's show these fresh kids up. Hey, gang?"

"Yeah. Let's go . . . let's go, gang!"

As soon as play commenced, they began to hit. Little by little they pulled up—32-34, 33-35—and finally the score was tied at 35 apiece. They were assured now; they felt they were in the driver's seat. You could hardly expect a veteran team to crack merely because they were behind six points at the half; and these boys, playing with poise and assurance, did not crack.

But the varsity didn't crack when they tied the score, either. Through the third quarter the kids played fine basketball. Strings was better than ever off the backboards, and Tom noticed with uneasiness that he was yanking the rebounds away from Red, a master of the art, time and time again. Coondog was fast, a hawk on a loose ball, but the stars were those pesky twins.

Tom admitted glumly to himself that he had forgotten how elusive they were, how hard to stop. Heads up, hands down, eyes always on the guard, they dribbled in past Ned and Joe, swinging the ball round, passing it, taking it back, ducking, feinting, faking, slithering past with a change of pace, always protecting the ball with their bodies. Tom tried playing Andy tight to prevent his passing. It was suicide, because he had such control of the ball.

So he passed the word around. Break this up. Stop Andy Davis. Two of them took over and stopped him cold. Immediately Randy broke loose.

There he went, that cowlick damp over his forehead, dodging Harry, outracing Joe, slipping the ball to Coondog, taking it back, passing it fast and true to Strings in the pivot, and shouting, "Hey . . . hey!"

Strings turned to Randy, flipped the ball quickly to Andy, took it back, and made a jump shot that hit cleanly. They just couldn't seem to miss. Slowly Tom began to realize this team was good; what had seemed liked luck from the stands last Saturday night wasn't luck at all. Things looked different out there on the floor when you faced those slippery kids yourself.

Basketball is tough on wind and legs, even for players fit and trained. The five veterans were neither. They had counted on their slow possession game, full of stalls and breaks, to give them command. Instead, they found themselves playing the hard-driving type of game their adversaries wanted. Moreover, the veterans had been without play for two months; now their edge began going and their shots became wild. As the last quarter came, slowly, minute by minute, condition counted.

In the last stages Strings was in command, out-jumping everyone off the backboards, coming down with the ball, swinging round, flipping it to Andy or Randy, who were off to the races.

Andy cut . . . Randy cut . . . passed . . . took the ball back . . . faked a pass, got round Joe and slipped the ball in over his head. Above everything Tom could hear that exasperating voice of Andy, coolly surveying the floor and shouting, "Spread out . . . spread out . . . spread out, you guys."

At this point Strings went out on fouls. The other four practically hugged him as he left the floor. His loss meant a big difference, but the margin was now 54-46. Tom watched Ned Spencer fight with Coondog for a jump ball; saw Coondog lose it, come down and steal it, and then, protecting it with his elbows, swing it across to Andy, who was off like lightning down the floor, the whole pack in pursuit.

The pound-pound of feet, the heavy breathing of the players, the hoarse shouts and cries rose in the heated gym. Tom felt blown. He was tired now and steaming, he was annoyed and upset, and so, he realized, were his teammates. With time running out it was agonizing to have those twins slip in and lay up another basket. Gosh, we gonna lose. We aren't gonna lose, are we? We can't lose to these kids. Surely we can't lose. To be the great Redskins, the former champs, and go down to defeat before the school hurt. With victory in the air, the other

team was now taking chances, going for the breaks
and getting them in every scramble for the ball.

The lucky rats, Tom thought bitterly.

Suddenly Hooks rose in the front row of the
balcony, blowing violently on his whistle. The
sound stopped them all, the pattern on the floor
dissolved, play ceased. Tom turned and shook hands
with Strings, who had rushed out to greet his teammates; then he slumped away, completely beaten.
Joe Boyd, panting, slapped Andy Davis mechanically on the back. Red turned his back on them all.
Heads down, the veterans moved dejectedly toward
the lockers where they had all dressed together
hardly more than an hour before.

The varsity rushed in after them, joyful and
jubilant. Yanking off their soaking shirts, they
waved them in the air.

"Hoo-ray for Strings . . . hoo-ray for Strings . . .
everybody here says . . . hoo-ray for Strings!"

"Hey there, Andy! Hey, Randy! Nice work,
great going, kids. Randy, you were sure hot out
there. Boy, you couldn't miss."

"You couldn't miss neither."

Exultantly they stripped off their wet shirts,
threw off their pants, and rushed for the showers,
yelling. If they had won the State they couldn't
have been happier. And their coach, who moved
quietly among them, couldn't have either.

But Tom and the other veterans sat motionless on the benches, heads between their hands, stunned and dismayed. Their easy defeat by Central City in the first game of the season could be laughed off. That crowd they could take any time by any margin. This game was different; now excuses were useless. The kids were hot; they were fast; they were good shooters; they hit and we didn't. What could you say? Nothing.

Defeat is always hard to take, but unexpected defeat is somehow worst of all. This was the chance they had wanted; this was everything they had hoped for, and to a man they had felt certain they would win easily. The chance had come, was there, and had vanished. They had muffed it.

None of them had even imagined the possibility of defeat. Consequently, they sat silent and motionless on those long, hard benches before the lockers. While from the showers came the sounds of running water and high-pitched voices, laughter and yells and shouts full of joy and meaning.

The former varsity heard nothing, saw nothing. They sat speechless, panting, their hair over their wet faces, sweat pouring down their necks and shoulders, unable to stir, to talk, to think. Yet in Tom's mind and in every mind was a horrible doubt.

Maybe . . . perhaps . . . we aren't as good as we thought we were!

Chapter 17

The horn sounded twice in his ears—imperious, insistent. As he looked around, a car drew up at the curb and Mary Jo leaned over from the driver's seat. "Tom! This is a break. Get in, please."

He stood hesitating. Not that he needed any urging; yet for just a moment he wanted to ignore her, to turn and walk off silently down the street. He felt a need to hurt someone to make up for the terrible hurt he had sustained that afternoon, which still rankled inside. Instead, he obeyed her and climbed into the car.

She drove rapidly down South Michigan in a purposeful way.

"What is it, a fire?"

"A fire? No. Worse."

"Oh. Where you going?"

"The Beverly Inn, out on the National Road."

The Beverly Inn was a famous roadhouse a few miles west of town on Route 40. Folks said you could play slot machines and put up money on the horses there if you wanted to. Everyone in town knew the Beverly Inn.

The car turned into South Maple, then left, onto the National Road. She leaned over and patted his hand. "I saw you slumping along there and decided to stop." He hoped she would make no reference to the afternoon, for that disaster was too deep inside to discuss. She never mentioned it. Instead, she said, "I need you, Tom. You'll help me, won't you?"

Her smile was appealing. Women—strange people, he thought. A few days before, she had been so angry with him because he asked her a simple question that she had stood up before 6000 people, every one of whom knew him, and called him a troublemaker and a sorehead. Now here she was, all smiles and warmth and charm, as if that meeting had never happened. Women were certainly peculiar. They threw a fellow off. He didn't know how to act. So he merely grunted. "What's up? What's cooking?"

"Red Blake. That's what's up."

He looked at her. "Red Blake? What's Red Blake to you?"

"Nothing. But twenty minutes ago I saw him go by in that old open car of his with the two Davis twins. Bet he's taking them to the Beverly Inn. Bet I'm going to find out, too."

"The Davis twins? The Beverly Inn? How's that . . . what's the big idea?"

"Don't you get it? Red takes those kids out there tonight, people see them, Hooks hears about it—trust Red for that—and throws them off the varsity like he did . . . like he did before. It's more of Red's strong-arm stuff. BB shots didn't work, so he tries a different angle."

"BB shots?" Tom sat up. So that was it. Red must have busted Hooks' windows and cut his tires. Of course it was Red! Now he remembered all the things Red had said about the coach. "So Red was the one?"

"You ought to know, Tom," she said quietly.

He turned on her furiously. "Me? You said that before. Look, Mary Jo, you know me better'n anyone. You really think I'd cut up a guy's tires and bust his windows?"

"But you said you had . . . you admitted it that night in the snow."

"I did nothing of the sort. I never said I'd done it. You accused me! You oughta know me . . ."

"Oh, Tom, honest, I'm so glad. I've worried so much. I felt sure you'd never play that kind of a game, never. Only you admitted it . . . sort of . . . that night."

"I tell you I didn't admit it." He was hurt and yet he was glad to be there with her in the car, too.

If Red shot up those windows, of course he splashed
Hooks' house with yellow paint, too. The pattern
was plain enough now. It had been happening right
under his eyes, and he had never seen, never guessed
who was at fault. Things were beginning to sort
themselves out. "Why, if Red shot up the windows,
he must have done the other things, too."

"Of course! How dumb can you be? Everybody
in town knows who did them, only there's no
proof. He's smart."

"Anyhow," said Tom stubbornly, "he never told
me."

"Ha!" She laughed. "Of course he never told
you! Think he'd tell the son of the mayor? He
knows a darn sight better than that. Besides, he
was sure you'd have something to say about cutting
tires and busting windows. He knew you'd be
burned up. Oh, Tom, I'm so glad to know, to be
sure you had nothing to do with those things. I
never really thought you had, only you sort of
admitted it that night."

"Look, Mary Jo, for the last time, I did *not*
admit it. You accused me of it; you shoulda known
me better, you really should've."

"Never mind now. There's the Beverly Inn up
ahead. If Red's car is there the Davis twins are there,
and if they are I mean to get 'em away somehow.
You've got to help me."

They slowed down and turned to drive into the parking lot. "Look," she said. "There's Red's jalopy, over there next to that Cadillac. It's just what I expected."

Tom had never been in the place and, as the son of the mayor, he did not need to be warned not to go there. Yet somehow he felt warm and happy to be pushing through the door with anyone as attractive as Mary Jo. Those were his thoughts, and they were shattered suddenly. A figure rushed past them, jumped into Red's car, slammed the door, and drove off.

It was Red Blake.

What's up? Where's he going? What's cooking? Tom wondered. Whatever happens, it probably isn't good. He began to see Red in a new and different light.

Then they were inside. The light was dim, the air was musty with tobacco smoke, the band in the corner was playing softly, and a few couples were dancing. Tom and Mary Jo stood hesitantly, looking around in the uncertain light, when a big figure in a dark suit bounced toward them. He was as broad as he was long.

"Good evening, Tom, glad to see you. Folks like a table?" he asked with assurance.

Because of his basketball, Tom was known to everyone in town, and the fact that the man called him by name was hardly surprising. This chap, he realized, must be the famous Mickey Rocco, owner of the inn, and not the best beloved or the most conservative citizen of Ridgewood.

"Thanks. We're looking for a couple of pals, Andy and Randy Davis. Maybe you've seen 'em, two kids with blue eyes and yellow hair."

"Sure. You mean those twins who came out with Red Blake? They're inside. Right this way." Tom realized immediately that by this time everyone in town knew the Davis twins. They had become Ridgewood's greatest attraction since the varsity had won the finals at Indianapolis the previous season.

Mickey opened a door and ushered them into a good-sized room, brightly lit and fairly well filled with people. This was the most famous room in town, and Tom had often heard folks talk about it. Everyone knew of its existence, and a good many men in Ridgewood knew about it to their regret. When Sam Blake was not hanging around Mac and Joe's Bar and Grill on Indiana Avenue, he was always out here at Mickey's.

On one side of the big room, all along the wall, was a kind of blackboard with a chart painted on it containing the names of the main race tracks throughout the country. In the center were tables with various gambling devices, and several card parties were in session. Around the wall across from the blackboard were a dozen slot machines; at two of them stood the Davis twins, engrossed in what they were doing.

"Hi!" said Tom.

They looked up, surprised, yet not at all embarrassed. They might have been drinking cokes in their father's store instead of playing the slot machines in the most notorious roadhouse in the county.

"Hello," they replied. Actually it was Tom, not the twins, who was embarrassed. The stares of the other clients at his pretty companion made him uneasy too.

"How you doing?" he asked, not knowing exactly how you addressed two members of the varsity in the inner room of the Beverly Inn.

"O.K. We're doing O.K.," said Andy with assurance, slipping a quarter in the machine.

Tom knew perfectly well that the Davis twins had no money. They earned what they got cutting lawns and shoveling snow; and until they made the B team both had had paper routes and delivered the *Sentinel* afternoons. Yet here they were pouring quarters into these machines as if they had been pennies.

"Look, you guys shouldn't chuck quarters away like that."

"Says who? Besides, we're not chucking them

away," replied Andy with some belligerence, as he yanked out the handle. "We're gonna win."

"That so? Maybe you're gonna lose. 'Nother thing you're gonna do—you're gonna get back home and get your sleep, not stay out here all night."

The cocky kid with the blue eyes looked up quickly. "It's not all night; it's not ten yet."

"It sure is! It's ten-thirty and you're breaking training."

"What's it to you?" asked Randy, in an unfriendly tone.

"Gee," interjected his brother, "you treat us as if we were ten-year-olds. Guess if we can make the Ridgewood varsity, we're old enough to have a little fun once in a while."

Just exactly the way I talked, thought Tom. That's how I must have sounded to my old man a few months ago. Now I'm sounding off like my father! Yet after all, the Davis twins were a couple of young fatheads; those two victories had been too much for them.

Then the horrible idea popped into his head that he must have sounded just as foolish when he had discussed Red, and Red's gambling at school, with his father. Not, of course, that he had been a fathead at the time, only . . .

Bong. Zoom. A cascade of quarters poured out in front of the delighted Randy. He scooped them up eagerly. "See? Leave us alone! Now we can go on with the game; we can go on all night, now."

"You're not going on all night. You're going home."

"No car," said Andy, with considerable truculence in his voice. "Gotta wait for Red. He's gone on an errand; he'll be back soon."

"We have a car. Look, you fellas," Tom pleaded. "Just suppose Hooks Barnum asks you where you were tonight." Once he asked me that question and I didn't like it, reflected Tom.

"Won't find out," replied Andy, stuffing another quarter into the machine.

"Yeah, sure, maybe not—only he will find out. That's his business, to know where the team is all the time."

"Aw, we just went for a ride with Red in his car. No law against that, is there?" asked Randy.

"No, but if he finds out you were here, out late, gambling, what about that? Plenty of folks here know you, and don't think they don't. This guy that owns the joint knows you."

"O.K. So we're gambling. Everybody in town does. We're not doing anything everyone in town doesn't do. You know that, Tom McWilliams. Just because your old man is the mayor . . ."

They were so exactly his own words. Only now he was his father talking.

"And besides," said Andy, "we gotta have some fun once in a while. We can't play basketball all day and all night."

"After next Saturday," said Tom firmly.

"After the 18th of March," replied Andy with assurance, meaning that the team would win the sectionals and the semifinals, and go into the finals on the 18th of March.

You stupid, swell-headed guys, Tom wanted to say. Yet once again the thought came that he himself must have sounded just like that a few months ago. So he said nothing.

Mary Jo, who hadn't said a word, who had merely stood there beside him, spoke now. "Look, boys, we have a car outside. Let's get moving." She smiled at them, and Tom wondered how anyone could resist her. But the twins had their eyes on the machines, not the girl.

"Nuts!" said Randy, without looking up.

"Naw!" said Andy.

"Yes," said Tom, with decision.

At the force in that single word they glanced up. Mary Joe came closer and took his arm. She could see the moment had come; she knew he meant business. So did the twins. They gazed at him, open-eyed.

"See here, you guys! I made a fool of myself last fall. I talked myself off the varsity and lost my final year of basketball. I'm not going to stand here and see you two make the same mistake. Will you come along with us now? Or what?"

He towered over them, tall, powerful, determined. They knew he could just about handle them both together if he got mad. Did he want to?

Andy looked at him closely, saw the big boy standing over him threateningly. Was it worth a scrap? He hesitated, glanced at Mary Jo, then at Tom, then shrugged his shoulders. "O.K. Just one more." He stowed a last quarter into the machine. Nothing happened. "Shoot!" he said with disgust, and turned away. "I was through anyhow."

They tramped back into the darkened room, refusing Mickey's offer of a table, and went out to Mary Jo's car.

"Gee," said Randy, "we didn't have any fun at all, at all."

"Wait a week. You can have all the fun you want after next Saturday," said Tom.

"After the 18th of March."

Tom merely laughed. He was happy to be there with Mary Jo close to him in the dark car, happy to have his misunderstanding with her over, happy to have pulled the twins away from the inn and perhaps done something for the team. Actually, before the car was more than a few yards down the road, they all realized that he really had.

Two state police cars scorched past, sirens blowing, headed for the inn. Behind, at some distance, was an ancient open Ford with Red muffled up in the driver's seat.

"Look! Hey, looka there! That's Red."

"Why, the dirty joker! He went for the cops. He must have told the sheriff these kids were out there. See if those cars turn in, Mary Jo."

She raised herself up in the seat and leaned over to peer out the back window. Red flashes appeared on the backs of the cars as they swung into the inn's parking space. There were certain things Sheriff Eikelberger would not tolerate in the county. Gambling by minors was one of them. So, with state police, he was raiding the joint.

Andy, who instantly realized the whole deal, let out a low whistle. "Whew, that was a close one." He turned to Tom. "Thanks, pal."

But Tom's mind was on Mary Jo, on her perception in seeing what had been taking place and her gameness in coming out to prevent it. He sat without speaking.

Then Randy spoke. "Yeah, thanks, pal, thanks a lot."

"Aw, shut up!" said Little Tom.

Chapter 18

Slowly and with reluctance Tom walked down the long hall. Here and there boys and girls spoke to him; he nodded, hardly hearing them. Out through the door he went, along the covered passageway to the field house, thinking of a remark of his father's, a remark from the distant past, half understood when first heard, now full of meaning.

The hardest thing in the world for a man to do is to admit he is wrong.

Yes, now I know what he meant. It's tough, but I was wrong. It wasn't really hard to say that to Mary Jo; she knew, she understood. This is different. Hooks may be sore after all that's happened. He may be certain I cut his tires and painted his house. This is the hardest thing I ever did in my life, harder than that last bucket in the finals last year at Indianapolis.

His feet dragged, his spirit sagged; he hated himself and longed to turn back, to chuck the whole idea. Yet something forced him to keep on, to enter the side door which he had gone through so happily and lightly so many afternoons on his way to practice; then through the familiar main lockers, with the battery of showers in the center, and out to the main hall of the field house. It was early. In fact, the last bell hadn't even sounded, the varsity had not arrived to dress, and only a few kids could be seen on the floor through the open doors. As he passed Hooks' little office he heard voices, so he went on, entered the hall, and sat down on one of the benches near the door.

The boys who were doing a little free-lance shooting all noticed him and increased the fury of their attack on the baskets, trying to show off before one of the old varsity veterans. Tom sat miserably alone, feeling exactly the way he used to before a big game, wishing things would start, wishing it was over and done with. Behind him, through the doors, he could hear people entering and leaving the coach's office. After a while the sound of voices ceased. He rose.

The tiny room, hardly big enough for the desk and two chairs, was empty. He turned, wondering where the coach could be with practice nearly due, wondering whether he had left the building temporarily to go downtown.

Then his strong, wide shoulders filled the doorway. "Hello there, Tom. How's tricks?"

"Hello, Hooks. I wanted to talk to you a minute."

"Come in. Sit down, boy." He closed the door and slumped into the chair at his desk, hands behind his head, leaning back, waiting.

Well, thought Tom, here comes the hardest part of all. Guess I'd better get it out; I'd better get it over and done with. "Hooks, I figgered . . . I mean I thought . . . I just came to say I was wrong. I was wrong all along about everything. Every one of us kids was wrong, but somehow I was the wrongest of all. I guess I had it coming to me."

Hooks leaned over and placed his hand on Tom's knee. "Thanks a lot, Tom. Y'know, I kinda hoped some day you'd see things this way. It's mighty fine of you, though, to come in like this and say it; takes a lot of courage, too. I know plenty of older men wouldn't do it. Tom, hope you know there was never anything personal about my decision. I simply had to do it even if it hurt and, believe me, it did hurt. You know what affection I had for you; we were mighty close last season."

Tom choked, thinking of the long year, the eternal practice sessions, the games with Hooks there on the bench, the tournament, and the finals, and how he hugged them all before the last half of the Fort Wayne game as they left the lockers, six points behind. How they all wanted to win for him. "Uh-huh. We sure were. Say, Hooks."

"Yes?"

"Hooks, I'm awful sorry now about those things, about the work I did on the petition and all. That darned thing—gee, I wish I'd never seen or heard of it."

"Forget it, Tom. I didn't mind. When a town gets stirred up about their basketball team, it shows they're really interested."

Hooks said that lightly enough, but Tom knew how the petition must have hurt him. Looking closely, he could see Mary Jo was right. The man had grown years older in the past few months. Now he noticed it plainly. Why, he wondered, did everybody see these things before he did?

"Hooks, you never thought I cut your tires or did those other things, did you? Hope not." He asked the question with anxiety in his voice.

The coach shook his head decisively. A faint smile came to his lips. "No sir, I never did. That ough stuff isn't like Little Tom McWilliams. Or Big Tom, either. That I knew. In fact, I was aware who did those things all along, and why."

"Now I know too. One fella did them."

"That's correct. And he was urged on by some shady characters downtown. Well, that's done, that's finished, that's all over like lots of other things. Now we must look ahead, not backward. We must all help the kids face up to these games on Saturday."

"Yes, Hooks. I came here for that reason, too. I'd like to help the team."

"Good! We need all the help we can get right now. Why don't you climb into your suit and come out this afternoon? You could do a world of good for Strings Johnson if you wanted to."

"I will. I sure will. Only one thing first. You know, better'n I do, that you'll never beat Marbletown next Saturday playing that fast-breaking game."

Hooks looked at him silently for a long while. "What makes you say that, son?"

"'Cause I've played against those boys—Rascin and Fellows and George Smith and the subs, too, all of them. I've met 'em two straight years now, ever since I was on the B team. I know exactly what they can do. I've felt them out on the floor; bet I know their strength and weaknesses as well as their own coach. Why, our gang would be worn out before the first half was over, and Marbletown would run away from them. They're all vets."

"Well, guess maybe so. But what . . ."

"Just this. With that slow game of theirs—those stalls and delays—they'll simply break up your running game. They've done it to better teams, to Tech last year, and Logansport and South Bend this

year. They love a fast break; they eat it. They're set
and ready for ours, too."

"I know. You're quite right. I've been awake
every night since Saturday thinking the same thing.
But I still haven't decided . . ."

"Here's an idea, Hooks, just an idea. Don't know
if it's any good or not. They're ready for our fast-
breaking game next Saturday night; they're all set
for it, aren't they?" The coach nodded. "Well,
suppose they don't get it."

Someone knocked firmly on the door. "I'm busy.
Come back later." Hooks sat up straight. "If I get
what you mean . . . think I see your point . . . only
it's tough on those kids of ours; we aren't really
suited to a possession game. Doubt if they've got
the patience and coolness you older boys had, even
if they could learn that sort of play."

"Why not? We'll work with them the rest of
the week. I'll work out on the floor with every man;
so will Harry and Ned and Joe. We want them to
win, Hooks."

"That's mighty fine of you boys. I appreciate it
lots. But look, son, we play Lafayette in the afternoon. If we play that slow game, George Eastlake
will adapt their style to it by evening. Marbletown
will be set for us."

"No, they won't," replied Tom quickly.

Hooks said nothing. He sat there staring. Now he saw the idea. It was dangerous. It was daring. It was risky in the extreme. Only a top-class, well-knit team could get away with it. The thing might not work. They might get badly beaten. And yet . . .

He sat motionless for a long, long while. The varsity had got into uniform, and you could hear the pound-pound of their feet, the slap-slap, slap-slap of balls on the floor as they passed through to the gymnasium.

"Wonder if you haven't got something there, Tom. Wonder if you haven't. As I get it, you mean to play our fast-breaking game in the afternoon; then, if we win, surprise Marbletown at night with possession ball."

"Right! That's right! That's it exactly, Hooks." Tom was excited himself now. The idea, he realized, was of course both difficult and dangerous. As an idea, though, it was brilliant. And he could help with the boys; he wanted to help. He knew he could help, too.

That little movement of Strings to the right before he pivots to throw—things like that a coach can hardly see, things you get to know from being out there on the floor with a man, his arms open, his body poised, ready to cut . . .

"Believe me, Hooks, I know that crowd over there. It's the only way in the world we can win Saturday."

The coach rose, shoulders back. "Tom, I believe you're dead right. I think you've got something there. It's so obvious I never saw it. We'll go out there today and start work on our slow game. Then if we come through in the afternoon we'll spring it on Marbletown at night. You'll have to help the rest of the week, Tom, and tell you what—on Saturday you'll sit on the bench beside me."

Chapter 19

Tom realized immediately that Hooks Barnum was putting on an act. It was a good act and he was an excellent actor, yet Tom saw how he felt. For although the coach talked in his usual quiet tone, pretending this would be just another game, he fooled nobody. It would be the regionals, the second step toward the finals.

It was Friday afternoon, the day before their biggest test. Hooks stood before them in the dressing room. "Bus leaves at ten sharp in front of the school. Anyone misses the bus, he doesn't get to play. Eat a big breakfast, late. We go on first, so we'll start dressing shortly after twelve. You fellows all know the Marbletown field house. This afternoon we'll have an hour's workout, mebbe an hour and a quarter. Loosen up carefully. Do some figure eights. Sharpen up your shooting. Randy . . . chuck in some foul shots. Make 'em good. Then we'll work real hard for half an hour on this slow game of ours."

Across the room Tom noticed Andy push his hair back from his forehead as he sat there on the bench in his sweat suit. He saw Coondog twist his fingers tensely. Every eye in the room was on the coach, who stood before them with a basketball in his hands.

"Like to say one thing. Marbletown has beaten us twice this year and on the record figures to be a better team than we are. Still and all, out on that floor records don't count. You boys been proving that lately, hey, Tom?"

Tom flushed slightly and nodded. "You're right, Hooks." The boys on the benches grinned; one or two even chuckled at the thought of that practice game with the former varsity. For the memory of their triumph was still sweet.

"Marbletown is a top-class team, a sound, well-coached team, and the only way in the world we can beat them is the way we've planned, the way we've talked over this week. We play the fast-breaking game we've used all winter against Lafayette in the afternoon. Then in the evening we go back to the deliberate game. When the Bearcats come out expecting us to run, we'll play possession ball. You hold onto it until a good scoring chance comes. A first-class team should be able to play either style, and hit that basket from anywhere, too."

Several boys on the benches shifted their weight. Tom knew they were worried.

So did the coach. "Yes, I know this is going to be hard for you. I'm asking what would be tough for a much more experienced team . . ."

"Isn't it risky, Hooks?" Shorty McCall's voice cracked ever so slightly.

He's the weak one. He's the one who'll break first, thought Tom. Every head was turned toward the coach, for this was a question in every mind.

Hooks jumped in. "I'll answer that. Yes, this is risky, mighty risky. But Tom knows those boys over there better'n any of us and he thinks it's the only possible way we can win. I agree. We're the underdog. We can afford to take chances; we must, that's all.

"Might be the Lafayette game in the afternoon will be your toughest fight, 'cause Marbletown will be all set for a fast-breaking game. They're bound to be surprised, not only by the shift in your style of play but because you aren't the same boys they licked earlier this year. They'll expect a soft touch and they won't get it. So they'll be thrown off; any team would be. They called us Barnum's Midgets. They all figured it was pretty funny we got past Central City. Well, they may all learn something.

They may find out we won that game on our merits.
If we get past the Broncos in the afternoon, I believe
we're in, I really do."

The visitors' dressing room in the basement of
the Marbletown field house was a cheerless place,
like most dressing rooms. There were rows of
benches with long stands beside them with hooks
and hangers for the team's street clothes. Across the
room were the showers, ten of them in a row.
Behind were the stairs leading up to the battlefield
above.

They tramped down, breathless, hot, weary, panting, followed by Jack Fields, the student manager,
the subs, and last of all by Hooks and Tom, who
was carrying the score book. The coach reached
the bottom of the stairs as the boys fell slumping
and sprawling onto the benches, heads down,
panting.

"O.K., gang. Relax! Just relax."

Hooks wandered around, then stopped nervously
beside Tom, who stood adding the fouls from the
score book. Hooks looked at the totals and then
turned to the benches. "Three on Strings. Watch
yourself out there this half, boy. Two on Coondog.
One on Andy, one on Randy."

Tom felt the man's tension as he walked nervously back and forth, his jaws moving on a wad

of gum. Jack Fields came down the line handing
out vitamin pills. Each player gobbled a couple.
There was silence over the room save for the heavy
breathing of the boys and their muttered remarks
to each other—brief comments on the game or the
style of their adversaries.

Then a door above slammed violently. There was
the pounding of footsteps on the stairs, a face leaning over the rail, and the shouted words, "Three
minutes!"

"Thanks, Norman." Tom could see how hard
it was for Hooks to keep the emotion out of his
tones and how he was struggling to master himself.
"All right, gang. Coondog, you're back in there
this half. Strings, back in for Lester. Now, gang,
six points is not enough to win this game, I . . . do
. . . not . . . believe. But if you keep playing the
way you've been doing, if you can hit that same
pace these next sixteen minutes, you'll come through.
I have every confidence in the world in you. Keep
moving, keep moving, keep moving, every second.
Andy, move to the strong side. Strings, you go
down, whenever you get that ball off the backboards. Any questions?"

He waited a minute, glancing at their set faces,
at the damp hair plastered over each twin's forehead,
at the tall colored boy glistening with sweat, at

Shorty McCall, the most vulnerable one of the five.

"O.K. Let's go."

"Let's go, gang, let's go!"

With a rush and roar they pounded up the stairs to the floor of the field house, where the whistle for the second half awaited them, to triumph or defeat.

A shriek greeted them from Block R as they took the floor. Mary Jo and the other yell leaders ran out in front of the stands.

"Let's *go* . . . Big Team . . . let's *go!*
You can win . . . Big Team . . . you *know* . . .
Let's *go* . . . Big Team . . . let's *go* . . . Big Team!"

When Tom passed down the side along the floor to his place on the Ridgewood bench, he noticed George Eastlake, the Marbletown coach, writing furiously at the press table. The sight made him happy.

The whistle blew, the ball was tossed. Strings slapped it back to Andy, and the crowd came up with a great roar that swept the arena. They loved this upset. They loved this driving, colorful basketball played by the Ridgewood team. They were excited and happy. Andy broke for the bucket, weaving in and out, dribbling in front and behind his back, caressing that ball without looking at it, passing, pivoting, taking it back. . . .

Suddenly there was a wild burst from the other side—and a groan from the Ridgewood stands. Lafayette had stolen the ball and was off slowly down the floor, trying to reduce the tempo of the game.

Tom, watching anxiously, was not fooled by their lead or the trend of the game so far. He knew the test was coming in the next few minutes. You have to be good to get to the regionals in Indiana, and Lafayette was a good team.

They had been off balance through the first quarter and had sunk only two baskets, while the Redskins poured in fourteen points. Then they had calmed down between the halves and now, with the score 30-24 against them, were fighting back desperately. They were covering the twins successfully, forcing Strings and Coondog to shoot from outside. Ridgewood was not hitting well, either.

"There! See that?" Tom grabbed the arm of the boy beside him. "He shot when he was off balance. Shorty was off balance then—no wonder he missed. Fellas get excited, they get overanxious. They let go when they shouldn't. Ah . . . nice work . . . nice screening on that one. Good work, Strings!"

The team raced down the floor past the Ridgewood bench, every face set and straining, every mouth open, the thud-thud of their feet pounding on the boards, their hoarse cries rising above the din.

"Hi . . ."

"Hey-hey . . . Andy . . . hey . . ."

"In here . . . in here . . ."

Suddenly the gun sounded for the end of the third quarter. Tom hastily added the figures, observing at once that they had been outscored since the first quarter. As he feared, this was still anyone's game to win.

It was 38-35 as they went into the final quarter, then 38-37. Lafayette was hot now. Both teams were all out, with the score 40-39 and half the quarter gone, when Strings fouled out. A sub raced in as the great giant came slumping onto the bench, hardly noticing when Lafayette hit from the corner to lead by a single point. It was the first time they had been ahead since the opening whistle.

Andy brought the ball rapidly down past the ten-second line, searching anxiously for an uncovered teammate. He turned and pivoted as he had done a hundred times that afternoon, but now he was tired, his reflexes were slower, and as he started to cut, his foot slipped and he tumbled to the floor.

Instantly an opponent pounced on the ball and was off to the races. The crowd rose, roaring, everybody on his feet. With less than two minutes to go, one bucket would sew it up for Lafayette.

The pattern on the floor shifted, changed, integrated and disintegrated a dozen times as the passes whipped back and forth, each Lafayette man waiting cautiously for an opening, for a sure chance at the bucket, for an unguarded spot on the court.

Tom ached. His whole frame suffered as he sat helpless on the bench, unable to do anything, unable to move, seeing the seconds go past. A minute and a half to go. A minute and a quarter. A minute. Less than a minute . . .

Then it happened. Coondog fairly leaped through the air, arm outstretched, batted down a pass, slapped the ball to the floor, scooped it up, and was off, pursued by nine frantic players. He was in the open, he was clear, he might have a shot . . .

Pray he doesn't travel, thought Tom. Pray he doesn't travel. Pray he doesn't hurry his shot . . . pray that kid behind fouls him as he shoots.

The ball went up, bounced on the rim . . . once . . . twice . . . fell through.

Ridgewood was ahead, 42-41.

Fifty-two seconds. Forty-five seconds, and Lafayette was across the ten-second line and down the floor. Thirty seconds, and the defense was holding. Twenty-five seconds, and a man darted in, was covered, turned, threw to a teammate beyond the foul line, who immediately pivoted and shot a one-hander.

The ball smacked the backboard with a thump. It bounced off directly into Andy's hands. He came down with it, swooped gracefully to one side, then to the other . . .

Ten seconds! Nine seconds! He passed to Randy. *Bang!*

The Redskins were facing Marbletown that evening.

Chapter 20

Ridgewood came out that night playing Barnum's famous control game instead of the firehouse basketball by which they had won in the afternoon. While the Marbletown players raced madly toward their goal to anticipate their opponents' lightning drive, Randy mooched down the floor, bouncing the ball deliberately, timing his progress to make it across the center line safely in the prescribed interval. Instead of driving into that tight defense, the Ridgewood players passed the ball casually among themselves, making no effort to go in.

These were surprising tactics to the Marbletown team, who expected a totally different style of play. They looked at each other uneasily, then at their opponents tossing the ball back and forth with exasperating calmness, performing in slow motion.

"Let's go get 'em," Rascin, the Marbletown center, muttered to his gang, and he ran toward

Randy, who was bouncing the ball slowly up and down.

But Coondog was edging to the far corner and Strings was easing into the pivot, while Andy and Shorty were crossing and coming to meet Randy. When Rascin was almost on him, Randy faked to Shorty, pivoted, passed to Andy, who bounce-passed through the Marbletown guard to Strings. The tall boy pivoted and sank the basket.

On the bench Tom was punching Hooks with excitement. "It's working. See how we sucked that defense out? D'ja see that?"

Twice in the first quarter Marbletown brought the ball down, took long shots, missed, and encountered that maddening offense from Ridgewood. They were piling up an unbelievable lead against this veteran team, picked as the number one tournament team. But Marbletown was composed of seasoned players and, once they got over the shock of frustration, they settled into a steady game. So there was slow, careful ball handling by both teams and little shooting. It was Barnum's control system against a more polished control game by Marbletown.

Up and down the floor the ball went, then back and forth, each side fencing for an opening, for an opponent's mistake that would let it move in. Each side scored and the quarter ended with Ridgewood on top, 11-3.

Marbletown scored first in the second quarter with a long shot. Then Rascin tallied a pair of charity tosses when Strings tried desperately to knock down his close-in shot. Randy netted one, but Marbletown immediately retaliated.

Slowly, relentlessly, the Marbletown veterans took command and pulled up until the score was tied at 18 all. Then a foul was called on Shorty.

For the first time, Tom understood how Hooks suffered during a game. Now he realized how it hurt to sit helplessly on the bench, unable to move, watching your team miss scoring chances and make mistakes. He was between Hooks and Jack Fields, the student manager. On each side of them were the subs, sweaters tossed over shoulders, arms folded, jaws chewing stolidly, a grim expression around every mouth.

Out on the floor, a Marbletown player in purple trunks bounced the ball coolly in that deep silence. Tom perceived the uneasiness of the Ridgewood team as they watched; he saw the fatigued look on their drawn faces. To his right, Mary Jo stood motionless before the stands, her hands at her lips almost in an attitude of prayer. Every player on the floor, everyone in the stands, knew this was the big moment.

The giant in purple bounced the ball again with a kind of proud arrogance, as if he knew he couldn't miss. Then, with the insolence of the veteran, his knees flexed, his arms went up, and the ball fell cleanly through the net. For the first time in the game Marbletown was ahead, 19-18.

The Ridgewood supporters sat silent and stunned. The Marbletown stands rose, shrieking with delight. "Get hot . . . team . . . get hot!"

The Bearcats *were* getting hot, too.

Tom was in agony. Occasionally he said something to Hooks. "They're riding Strings under that basket. They're covering him from head to foot."

"Right. They've got two men on him now. Why doesn't Andy get in there?"

The little towhead was directly opposite them now. An opponent stood in front of him, arms wide, stamping his feet, shouting. Tom realized how much coolness it took not to make a hurried shot and a bad pass at moments such as these, and he began to see there were two fine teams out on the floor, each with respect for the other's ability and courage.

But Marbletown was a tough team and a tall one. George Eastlake, their coach, always had a lot of big boys. There was a story that he "grew" his kids in grammar school by making them wade out into the Marble River each spring when it was full, until they had to stretch to keep from drowning. They were tall, and their shooting was uncanny.

Moreover, as the game progressed, Strings Johnson became less effective. All that day he had been a rubber-legged center off the backboards, snaring the rebounds and never giving the other side more than one shot at the basket. Tom watched with admiration, remembering the big giant when he first came out for practice, so clumsy he could hardly run from one end of the court to the other without falling down. But Marbletown was ready for him; they gave him a battering under the basket and stopped him cold.

Throughout the second quarter the teams fought stubbornly, neither more than a basket ahead. Then came the dying moments of the half, the last seconds ticking away, and with them, disaster. Rascin, the enemy center, stole a pass, drove under, and hit. He was fouled by Randy, made his first free throw, and missed the second. The score was 27-23, with Marbletown leading, as the two clubs walked off the floor panting, heads down, while the stands rose, yelling.

In the dingy locker room the Redskins sat slumped on the bench in attitudes of fatigue and disappointment. As he came down behind them, Tom instantly knew how they felt; he saw how beaten they were after that game of racing, tearing basketball in the afternoon. Instead of having a comfortable lead, they were behind. No coasting now. Nothing easy ahead. Uphill going all the way for a weary, exhausted squad.

He passed among them between the benches, handing Randy a towel, adjusting Shorty's ankle brace, patting Coondog on the shoulder, saying a word to Andy. The gang sat there muttering to themselves, despair in their tones.

"Aw . . . I didn't foul him . . . I didn't."

"Nope. He fell a-purpose."

"They're good, them boys are."

They sat panting, chins in their hands, not saying much. Strings slumped over, his depression plain in the set of his bony shoulders. Andy's head was down; Randy frowned as he sopped his brow. Shorty McCall rose to change his soaking shirt for a dry one.

Tom ran his hands through Andy's hair, slapped the big colored boy on the back. "Nice work on those backboards, Strings. You really go up there and get 'em. Stay with it now, stay with it, and when you come down with the ball don't forget your fakes. We'll be all right this half; it's our fakes and drives—that's where the trouble is."

No one spoke, no one responded. They had no voice and little heart to reply. Hooks came toward them. "Two on Andy . . . one on Randy . . . two on Shorty . . . Strings, you got three. Watch yourself. Don't feel down, guys, you did all right; you played well. That's one great team up there. But they haven't shown Tom and me they're the best, have they, Tom?"

"*No sir.*" Tom's tone was direct and emphatic. One or two faces along the benches glanced up now as he continued. "Nothing proves they're a better team. Sure they're tough. They hadda be tough to get here. I know how tough they are, betcha life I do; I played against 'em last year. But you fellas are going good. All's necessary is to cut out a few mistakes, believe me. That's all in the world you have to do to win."

The bitter, disappointed expressions were less noticeable now. For this wasn't the coach talking; it was Little Tom, one of them, a guy who had been through the same grind, who knew what it was to face a team like the Bearcats on their own floor. "Now, look," Tom continued. "Look, you men. Remember how they all called you Barnum's Midgets back in January, and asked how you ever got past Central City, and said what a laugh you were as a team? Remember? Here you are, and this team is scared. They don't like having you on their tails this way; they know this game isn't won yet."

"Now let's get down to cases," Hooks said, glancing at a sheet of paper with notes on it. "The defense on the weak side is sucking us in. Swing that ball, Strings, when you come down; swing that ball, man, swing it wide and swing it true. You know how. Shorty, get your head up! Work those corners. Shoot in front of him once in a while. Coondog, nice screening on Andy's two last goals; nice work there.

"Now you were all told what smooth ball handlers they were; you sure found that out the end of the last quarter. Randy, they just about faked you to death then. Watch Rascin this half; watch his eyes every second—he shows when he's ready to give and go. That boy is mighty fast; he can drive in. They've been doing most of the moving so far."

Suddenly an excited voice came down the stairs. "Hey, Hooks! Hey there, Hooks! Marbletown has an oxygen tent in their dressing room."

Everyone looked up, alarmed. An oxygen tent! Is that right? Is that fair? Won't that give them a big advantage? Everyone looked to Hooks to see what he would say.

Turning his head, he called back. "Fine! They'll need an oxygen tent and more, too, before we finish with 'em tonight. See that, fellows, an oxygen tent! That's what they think of you. Tom told you they were scared; this proves it. Now then . . ."

Another voice from above shouted. "Two and a half to go!"

"Thanks, Norman. Well, there isn't a whole lot

to say. All we were getting those last four minutes was a little figure eight before the basket. That's no good. Andy, you know that. Coondog, you know it too. How many times must I tell you not to shoot when you haven't a good opening? They've been hitting from way out; they won't this half. Whatever happens, don't you shoot unless you have a chance. Hold that ball, Shorty; the longer you keep it away from them, the less chance they have to score.

"Get it in to Strings like you did this afternoon. Those two boys can't handle him if you give him any kind of a pass. Get it in high to the pivot man; he'll hit every time.

"O.K. I believe you'll come through. I honestly think you have the stuff to do it. Look, you were further down than this at Fort Wayne; they led us 40-22 the end of the half that night. See how far you've come. The pressure is on them; that's the reason for the oxygen tent—they've got to clean up this half. If you don't make mistakes, I know you'll win. Tom, anything to say?"

Everyone glanced up as Tom towered above them. He had played these guys; he understood how hard it was to come from behind when your legs hurt and your lungs ached, when you had to go on and on. When you had to give a little harder, a little more than you'd ever given before. Yes, Tom had been there himself. So they listened.

"Fellas, we've all had some tough times this year, you, and I, and Hooks—every one of us in Ridgewood basketball. But win or lose, you fellas have nothing to worry about. You've come out all right. You're up there when folks in town were sure you couldn't do it. When everybody laughed at you." He paused, and his head dropped a little. "And I laughed along with the rest."

The silence was intense over the room. They could see how sorry he was for what had happened, and how wrong he had been; and they also felt they had been the ones to show him his mistake, to make him eat his words. Heads rose, faces became suddenly alert and alive. You could see their discouragement vanish, their faith return, their confidence come back.

"Well, just about the whole town was wrong, like I was. You've showed Ridgewood. You've proved it to the whole state. Everyone quit on you except one person—Hooks Barnum. Now, you guys, you have sixteen rough, tough minutes up there. Don't quit on him."

The benches scraped on the concrete floor; the team rose yelling. "Yea, gang . . . yea . . . Ridgewood . . . let's go, gang . . . let's go get 'em!"

There was the sound of husky, confident voices, and two steps at a time they rushed up toward the door to the arena above.

Chapter 21

As they worked their way through the crowd, Tom in the rear with Hooks at his side, the loudspeaker was booming away.

"Dr. Ralph Kellogg. Dr. Ralph Kellogg, please check at the front entrance."

"Will the owners of Indiana KK 5877 and KM 379 kindly remove their cars? They are blocking the parking lot."

"Mrs. L. F. Miller, please report to the east door at once."

Suddenly the two sides of the arena erupted as the teams took the floor, basketballs in their hands. There was a little throwing at the baskets, a little loosening up. The official timekeeper seated at the press table down front, with a dozen electric switches before him connecting the two big scoreboards at each end, flipped his numbers to check them. The referees, in gray trousers and black-and-white shirts, one with a ball under his arm, appeared.

Strings Johnson and big Rascin for Marbletown stepped to the center circle. The colored boy turned, looked carefully to see where his teammates were placed—at Andy, at Randy, at Shorty and Coondog. The referee stood with one hand in the air holding the ball, his whistle at his lips.

"Ready . . . ready . . ."

Strings leaned over slightly. The whistle sounded, the ball rose in the air. He leaped and batted it into Randy's arms, while all Ridgewood came up with a roar.

Randy calmly passed to Coondog, who pivoted, got under, shot, and missed a one-hander. But Strings retrieved the ball and then the team caught fire.

Andy potted a hand-out, then Strings hooked in a set shot, and the Redskins went ahead on Shorty's lay-up after a drive underneath. Sitting nervously on the bench, Tom realized this game was not going to be easy for either side.

As Ridgewood took the lead, 29-27, and the Bearcats brought out the ball, Mary Jo danced to the center with the other yell leaders. "Hey . . . hey . . . whadda ya say . . . let's get that ball away!"

Above, Block R was in perpetual motion, one row bending to the right, the row behind swinging far to the left at the same time, always moving, calling, imploring, yelling the team to victory. They

groaned when Fellows, of the Bearcats, got loose
and hooked the ball in to even the score. They
shouted as Andy came down the floor with the ball.

"We gotta win . . . let's go . . . We gotta win
. . . let's go . . ."

Tom watched the little chap pass the ten-second
line, belligerence in every move of his body. Andy
was the most dangerous man on the floor. He tor-
mented and tantalized the Bearcats with his blinding
speed and got his shots away so quickly he was
hard to cover. Whenever they played him tight,
he had such body control and balance that he kept
sliding past the guard and under the basket.

The going got tougher, scoring more difficult;
the defenses were tight, because points were vital
now and a mistake could mean the game. When the
third quarter ended, Ridgewood had a slender 38-34
margin with eight minutes of play left.

But Marbletown was a great team. Tom knew
they would strike back, and strike they did. Sinking
two long shots from way out on the floor at the
start of the fourth, they evened the score at 38
apiece. Again Strings, from the pivot, took Randy's
pass, turned, and slipped the ball in, his arms almost
up to the level of the basket; again the Bearcats
evened it up with a long shot from the corner. It
seemed to Tom, as he watched the ball plop in, that

these boys couldn't miss. They hit from thirty feet as easily as if they were under the basket.

Four minutes to go, then three left, as Randy stood there with the ball, ducking and feinting. This, as Tom knew, was where experience and game-toughness counted. With the clock ticking off the seconds and the whole crowd on their feet yelling, this was the place for a young team to crack. Tom watched each man with attention, speaking occasionally to Hooks at his side, praying now for steady hands, cool nerves, and keen eyes. Three to go, the teams tied, and Ridgewood trying vainly to break through the steely defense around the basket.

"We wanna bucket . . . we wanna shot . . . we wanna score . . . get hot . . . get hot!" implored the Ridgewood stands.

There goes Andy! Protecting the ball with his body, dribbling eight inches from the floor, head up, eyes on his adversary, that wet strand of yellow hair over his forehead, the little chap darted to left and right, trying to slip in. But he was a team player; suddenly he slipped the ball to Randy, who passed to Coondog, who faked and turned and passed back to Andy.

Now two Marbletown men were on Strings every minute. So Andy faked a pass to him, pivoted, and went in . . . he was nearly under . . . he handed

it off to Shorty, whose guard was screened by Strings
and who had a clear shot. He tossed it up.

The ball fell through. 42-40.

But there was a whistle on the play. The referee
raced over, pointing out a Marbletown man who
had fouled. Instantly Tom saw George Eastlake,
their coach, charge across the floor, calling on his
players, shrieking at the referee, addressing the
heavens, waving his arms in a furious frenzy.

It was a terrific act, worth absolutely nothing.
Remorselessly the referee handed the ball to Shorty
McCall. Everyone in the place knew two points
would put the game on ice.

Silence fell over the stands. Suddenly the loudspeaker boomed out. "Found—a pair of spectacles.
Owner please check at the east-gate ticket office."

"Give 'em to that referee," shouted the Bearcat
stands, almost in unison. A laugh rose which broke
the tension momentarily. Everyone smiled save
Shorty, bouncing the ball nervously before the
basket.

He stood with the ball for what seemed to Tom
a million years. He's afraid, he's scared, he thought;
he hates to throw, he knows how much depends
on it. Hang it all, if only that was Andy, the money
player, or Randy or Coondog or Strings. If only it
wasn't Shorty, the nervous, sensitive type, who feels
things, who's too strung up at a time like this . . .

He threw at last. As he started his throw, the Bearcat stands rose, yelling. Everyone could see it was high, wide, and not handsome. The ball hit the backboards and bounded away.

"If only that hadda been Andy . . ."

"Anyone but Shorty. He's much too tight to hit now," responded Hooks.

You could feel his tightness as he took the second ball from the referee. His shot was high above the hoop, and Nichols, a Marbletown player, leaped to snare it off the backboards.

Now everyone was up yelling wildly, calling incoherently for a basket for Marbletown or imploring Ridgewood to hold. Two minutes and a half to go! A hundred and fifty seconds left! The clock moved so slowly, so calmly, for Ridgewood; so rapidly, so brutally for Marbletown. The Bearcats were desperate. They had to hit once to tie the score.

Then a whistle blew. Time out. Marbletown sent in another sub; but Hooks had only weak replacements and had to go with his exhausted five. They huddled together at the side, Hooks and Tom bending over their sweaty, heaving backs.

"Hold 'em, guys . . . hold 'em, keep that defense tight . . . make 'em throw from out there . . . they'll start missing . . ."

Across the way the thunder from the Bearcat stands drowned out his words. "Go on . . . go on . . . that's all right . . . come on, Bearcats . . . fight . . . fight . . . fight!"

The raucous horn called the teams to position. Rascin took the ball out quickly. Two minutes and ten seconds to go. Everyone had one eye on the big electric clock overhead. Rascin came in, pivoted, passed, turned away, playing slowly and carefully, trying to make the shot a safe one, to break a man open under that basket.

Seventy seconds. One minute. Fifty seconds. A frenzy rose over the arena as Rascin suddenly pivoted and threw from the left side. The ball went through with a sickening swish. The score was tied!

Andy brought it out quickly, eyes on the clock above, crossed the ten-second line, tossed the ball to Coondog, took it back again, shot another glance at the clock, flipped it to Randy, who faked to Strings, and then, with only a few seconds left, the big colored boy threw from the outside.

The ball was wide and a scramble on the floor ensued.

Bang! The gun sounded. The score was tied at 42 each, and the game was going into an overtime period.

Chapter 22

As the overtime began, Tom perceived that both teams were handicapped. Ridgewood had an inexperienced and exhausted team on the floor; they were playing on courage alone. Yet their control game was so perfect that Marbletown, fearful of fouling, had to stand back and wait for the breaks.

The first break came when Strings missed the tip-off and Marbletown drove under the basket. Fellows was fouled by Coondog and stepped to the line in an atmosphere of frenzy. He showed the pressure plainly, missing the first shot and sinking the second to put the Bearcats ahead by a single point.

Andy came back with the ball quickly, flipping it in to Strings, then working clever blocks and smooth hand-offs to send Coondog and Shorty under the basket. At last Shorty got free, received the ball, and shoved in a one-hander with a minute and a half to go. This put Ridgewood ahead by a single point, 44-43.

Unfortunately, a few seconds later Strings fouled Rascin as he came under, and was out of the game on personals. The big colored boy, shaking off the congratulations of his teammates, came to the bench in tears, chucking his jacket over one shoulder and slumping down next to Tom. Half a dozen players rushed across to shake his hand but he was heartbroken. There he sat, head down, sobbing, as Milton King, his sophomore sub, rushed eagerly out onto the floor.

Amid a tense silence Rascin shot and made the first one, to tie the score at 44 apiece. He took a long while over the second—too long, perhaps—and missed. The score was still tied, with only a minute left.

A mass of arms reached for the ball under the basket. Shorty finally grabbed it from an opponent, ducked low, pivoted, and snapped to Randy. Now Randy came down the floor, past the ten-second line, flipped the ball to Coondog, who mechanically eyed the clock reeling off the red seconds above. He passed to Andy, who vainly tried to crack the sturdy Bearcat defense. Fifty seconds. Forty seconds. Thirty seconds. Twenty-five . . . twenty . . . fifteen . . . and every man on the floor counting them to himself. Randy to Shorty . . . a bounced pass to Milton King in the pivot, who dribbled a few steps and threw.

The ball struck the rim cleanly, rolled round . . . and round . . . and fell away.

A shriek, a mighty roar from one side of the arena, a groan from the other as Marbletown snatched the ball in the melee under the basket and tried to get a final fling at the bucket. Then suddenly the pistol cracked. The overtime was ended and the score was still a tie.

Sudden death, the ending prescribed by tournament rules for a second overtime, was all that remained. When one team succeeded in making two points the game would be automatically ended. This period is timeless, the end certain—and quick. An opening, one lucky shot, and all is over. One team emerges triumphant to enter the Sweet Sixteen for the State semifinals; the other, defeated, returns to obscurity and lifelong dreams of what might have been.

The atmosphere was explosive, the tension unbearable. Tom dug his nails into his palms and shut his eyes. High up in the stands, a girl screamed, while another nearby slowly slipped to the floor in a faint. For a moment nobody noticed her. Then a companion shrieked, "Get a doctor!" It seemed as if the crowd could stand no more. Or the players, either.

The Marbletown team was in a tight little cluster at one end of the floor, Ridgewood at the other.

A shrill whistle sent a tingling down Tom's back-bone. His eyes burned as he saw the players move toward the center circle—for the last time.

"Go, team . . . go! Go, team, go! Go, team . . . go!"

Mary Jo stood with the other three yell leaders in front of Block R, watching. No need to lead yells now and, for that matter, impossible, for everyone in the Ridgewood stands was up, pounding with their feet, shouting in unison. "Go, team . . . go! Go, team . . . go!"

Ridgewood got the ball at the tip-off, but Shorty fumbled a pass. Luckily Coondog was alert; he pounced upon it and was off down the floor. But he double-dribbled, and the ball went to the Bearcats in a frenzy of noise from all over the arena.

There! See that! Rascin is coming down, searching for a free man.

The ball zipped around the Bearcat arc, while the Redskins, mouths open, arms up, darted in and out, working for a break of any kind—a bad pass, any-thing to get the precious possession necessary for scoring.

Suddenly the ball came back to Rascin, who stood motionless with the coolness of the veteran. He would try no desperation shot at the basket, for now every move counted, and no one could take chances. Then, sensing an opening, he slammed in underneath, cut out to the corner, pivoted, and came back, but as he turned, he hit Shorty McCall and sent him spinning to the floor.

Instantly there was a whistle on the play. The foul was called on Rascin. Two free throws for Shorty!

The two squads unraveled slowly in a furious uproar. "Go, team . . . go! Go, team . . . go . . . Go, team! . . . Go!" urged the Ridgewood stands.

Tom watched with a sinking feeling as they walked down to the opposite basket. This could be it, this could win as Shorty should have won before. But why did Shorty always have to be the man? Why did everything always depend on Shorty? Why couldn't we get a break for a change? If only it was Andy, or Randy, or Coondog, or even Milton King out there . . . or Strings.

Mac and Joe's Bar and Grill back on Indiana Avenue was so jammed that night there wasn't an extra inch of space. No one could get in anyhow, because the front door had been locked. The pool tables in the rear were deserted. The crowd was packed in the front room, standing six deep around the bar, jamming the booths and sitting on the tables in the center. Every eye was on the television set. All you could see was a tense figure bouncing the ball nervously before the Marbletown basket. All that could be heard was the roar from the Ridge-wood stands. "Go, team . . . go! Go, team!"

The noise subsided as the boy stood motionless, head down, rolling the ball around nervously in his fingers. You could see the strain he was under in the set of his body, in the way he tightened his face and shoulders as he looked up solemnly, flexed his knees, came up with the ball, and threw.

It smacked the backboards with a thud, fell back, and rolled cleanly through the hoop.

The room dissolved in noise. One point and one to go! This is it! This is the big one! This is the one that counts, the money point. If he makes this . . .

The boy took the ball almost reluctantly from the referee, almost as if he didn't want to touch it. Again he stood endlessly poised, trying to summon up reserves of courage. Again his head was down; again he rolled the ball nervously in his hands. Silence fell over the arena. Even the announcer was silent for once. Then at last his knees bent and the ball came up suddenly, as though he could not stand the tension any more.

The crowd never saw it fall through; all they could see was the bedlam on the floor. A Marble-town player dropped to the boards sobbing. The excited Redskins waved their arms and surrounded Shorty, and the mob rushed from the stands.

Back in Mac and Joe's Bar and Grill, the room dissolved into utter confusion, everyone cheering, shouting, screaming for Ridgewood.

"Doggone, they done it again."

"What d'you think of that? The kids came through again!"

"So . . . Ridgewood will represent this section in the semifinals next week," shouted the announcer over the noise and tumult from the arena in Marble-town. "The crowd is surging onto the floor now.... It's a wonder those boys aren't crushed to death in that mob. . . . Listen to the girls of Block R! Yes, the Redskins came through again, they sure did . . . and we've just had a flash, folks; Fort Wayne Central won their regional this evening, so they'll face Ridgewood in the first game next Saturday afternoon in the semifinals.

"Hey, there comes a stepladder. Strings is the first one up . . . hear that gang yell for him! Here comes Andy Davis . . . he's cutting off a piece of the net . . . and there goes Shorty McCall . . . what a cheer he's getting from the crowd! Now Randy is up . . . and Hooks Barnum is cutting himself a slice and . . . Who's this? They're pushing someone up there . . . It's Tom McWilliams, who sat on the bench and helped plan the Redskin strategy all day. He's up there now! Oh, they'll tear the town apart tonight. . . ."

MacDonald, owner of the Bar and Grill, worked his way with some difficulty through the jubilant crowd and squeezed out toward the front of the room. He had a large, floppy piece of white paper in one hand. To prevent it from being crushed, he held it high above his head. When he had finally pushed through to the window, he shoved aside a low curtain hanging on a rail, reached over, and yanked out a faded, dusty placard which read *Sign the Petition*. This he crumpled up and tossed to the floor behind him. Next he leaned over and pasted the white paper in his hand to the outside window. It was a three-word sign: *Win the State!*

Chapter 23

Meanwhile, down in the dressing room at Marbletown pandemonium reigned. A kid beat a bass drum, but its booming was lost in the noise and turmoil. Andy waved his shirt like a banner over his head. Strings went from one to another, hugging each player on the team. Everyone was laughing and shouting and yelling, chucking towels about, whooping and calling to each other, going over those final minutes of the last overtime, reliving those agonizing moments when they played with disaster at their heels every second.

Then all at once the chant rose, clear and spontaneous. "Sectionals . . . regionals . . . semifinals . . . finals. Sectionals . . . regionals . . . semifinals . . . finals!"

The photographers poured down, crowding the team and the subs together on benches in the center of the room. Now big Strings waved a portion of the tattered net, Coondog's neck had a collar of white strands, and Randy and Andy raised fistfuls in the air. Behind them stood Hooks, radiant at last, beaming, free and loose for a moment.

"Tom! Hey there, Tom! Little Tom!"

"Tom, c'mon in here."

He stood at one side, shaking his head. After all, it was their show. They had done it, won it, taken it away from the toughest team in the state all alone on that court. Then he noticed his father's big shock of hair above most of the other heads in the crowd.

Voices kept calling. "No . . . wait a minute . . . wait for Tom." "Hey, Tom, get in there. You're part of the team."

Somebody yanked his arm, somebody else pushed him, and there he was at the end of the second row, pressing close to Andy's sweaty body. The photographer held up his camera with the flash bulb at the side.

"Now, boys, give us a big yell."

"Let's *go*, big team . . . let's go!"

"Indianapolis . . . here we come!"

"Let's go . . . big team . . . let's go!"

Then the cheering group dissolved. Hilarious and excited men poured down the stairs: Mr. Hitchcock, the principal; Mr. Schroeder, the superintendent of schools; half a dozen reporters; several Redskin veterans of other years. Standing back, on the edge of the excited throng, Tom watched his father work his way through the circle about the coach. He knew this was one man Hooks Barnum was really glad to see.

They shook hands, grinning; spoke briefly. Tom could see Hooks smile and nod; then the circle of reporters closed in around him. He could just make out the coach's voice in the uproar.

"Why, yes, Bill, we planned it that way. Risky . . . you're right; sure it was risky. Well, maybe we were a little lucky at times, but it was our only chance. Fact is, the idea wasn't mine. Little Tom thought it out; he knows those Marbletown boys better'n any one of us. It was all his idea."

Several reporters turned to look at him curiously. Then somebody dashed down the stairs, shouting, "Marbletown has closed their dressing room. They won't see anybody."

This caused little excitement. Nobody wanted to see the Marbletown team; that night everybody was interested in Ridgewood. How did they do it? How had Hooks managed to make a team out of the gang that everyone called Barnum's Midgets?

"Well, Tom." He heard his father's voice in his ears. "Well, son, I rather guess, from what they say, that congratulations are due you as much as anyone."

Little Tom couldn't take that, because he knew only too well what it meant to come from behind in a tough fight—what it was like to be out on that floor with the pressure on you, to be beaten and bushed, the calves of your legs solid lead, your whole body aching with fatigue. He knew so well how a man felt when they handed him the ball and he had to hit. When the whole season hung on two free throws, and 16,000 fans held their breath, and you saw nobody and nothing save that bucket up there and the white strands hanging down.

He protested quickly. "No, Dad, I just sat it out. I sat there and suffered same as you did. Like everyone else."

"Maybe. Then again, might be you did more for that bunch tonight than you ever did as a player on the floor. That was a great win, and I'm proud of you, boy, a good deal prouder than I was last year, even." He hung one long arm over Tom's shoulders.

"Thanks, Dad. That means a lot. Say, it's started to snow. What say we get going? We have a long, slow ride in that storm. Let's us get moving."

"Aren't you staying to eat dinner with the team?"

"Nope. I've just about had all I can take. I'd like to get started for home when you're ready."

They turned and went up the stone stairs, leaving the hilarious dressing room, and into the corridors above. The crowd had thinned out perceptibly, but there were still numerous friends and relatives of the players standing around. A dozen people called to Tom; many spoke to the mayor as they made their way slowly through the exit toward the street. They reached the big double doors, and Tom found himself carried along into the whirling snow outside. He stood waiting, his hands in his pockets, until his father, the center of a small group just inside the door, could break away.

Then Mary Jo came out through the double doors, looking to both sides, searching behind her in the hallway. Her hair hung over her shoulders. She wore her white costume with the big red *R* on the white sweater and the white skirt and saddle shoes in which she had led the yelling all day. Suddenly she saw him through the glass doors, standing alone in the snow by the curb. She rushed through, and as she approached he reached out, grasped her under the shoulders and yanked her off her feet and into his arms.

For a while she hung there, while the people still pouring from the doors turned curiously, watching. One small boy gave a wolf whistle but several others standing nearby jumped on him.

"You creep! That's Mary Jo Berry! She's Little Tom's girl!"